'It's all abve,
not Jas ar is
killing it –
'Don't sp ce
growing stern.
'I don't care any more,' I told her. 'As soon as I can,
I'm out of here. You can keep your stupid views about
honour. I'm gonna find out .what happened to Jas
without you – any of you!'

PRAISE FOR BALI RAI:

ıeart-rending tale from a talented author'

The Times on *City of Ghosts*

**ılliant piece of original writing, this novel is
ıought-provoking and hugely readable'**

The Bookseller on *(un)arranged marriage*

'A jewel of a book'

Independent on *The Crew*

www.totallyrandombooks.co.uk

Bali Rai

KILLING HONOUR

CORGI BOOKS

KILLING HONOUR
A CORGI BOOK 978 0 552 56211 9
First published in Great Britain by Corgi Books,
an imprint of Random House Children's Books,
A Random House Group Company
This edition published 2011
1 3 5 7 9 10 8 6 4 2

The Random House Group Limited supports the Forest Stewardship Council (FSC),
the leading international forest certification organization. All our titles that are
printed on Greenpeace-approved FSC-certified paper carry the FSC logo.
Our paper procurement policy can be found at www.randomhouse.co.uk/environment.

Mixed Sources
Product group from well-managed
forests and other controlled sources
www.fsc.org Cert no. TT-COC-002139
© 1996 Forest Stewardship Council

Set in Din

Corgi Books are published by Random House Children's Books,
61–63 Uxbridge Road, London W5 5SA

www.**kids**at**randomhouse**.co.uk
www.**totallyrandombooks**.co.uk

Addresses for companies within The Random House Group Limited can be found at:
www.randomhouse.co.uk/offices.htm

THE RANDOM HOUSE GROUP Limited Reg. No. 954009

A CIP catalogue record for this book is available from the British Library.

Printed and bound in Great Britain by CPI Bookmarque, Croydon, CR0 4TD

*A massive thank you to Ruth Knowles and
the RHCB editorial team for helping to turn
a good idea into a great story.*

*An even bigger dedication to Philippa,
Annie, Sue and everyone @ RHCB for ten
wonderful years of hard work and support.
Big kiss to you all – past and present!*

*The same goes for Penny and Jennifer Luithlen
for being the best agents in the world. xxx*

*And finally to everyone else who has supported me
over the years – the readers, librarians, bookshops
and others who make my job amazing. Cheers!*

The room is cold because she's left the window open, and a wintry storm has turned the sky purple. The wind sneaks in and stabs at her with its icy fingers but she doesn't notice. She's in an unmade bed, in the dark; lying to one side, her legs curled up so that she resembles a ball. The tears have stopped running down her face but the pain in her belly refuses to go away . . .

He'd come to her earlier, sniffing and coughing, with bulging eyes and drunken lust. Pushed her down and taken what he wanted, as always. He'd been violent, meeting each of her cries with a slap or a pinch; or by yanking at her hair so that her scalp burned. In the end she'd let him have his way, whimpering as he'd subjected her to yet another humiliation. Relieved once she'd heard him grunt like an animal, clean himself with a tissue, pull up his jeans and leave.

'Useless little bitch!' he'd sneered. 'What's the point of you?'

She turns on her other side, her head pounding. A trickle of warm fluid makes its way down her thighs. She reaches down, brings her hand to her face.

Menstrual blood coats her fingers. She retches twice before running to the bathroom and vomiting into the toilet bowl. Little explosions of light, like fireflies, zip across her field of vision. The bile in her throat makes her gag, and she wonders whether other wives go through the same thing. Is this what married life is all about?

The journalist looked at me across the coffee shop table as an elderly couple walked past. We were sitting in Caffè Nero, close to St Pancras station. I ignored her gaze and pretended to people-watch. It didn't work. I looked back into her face.

'Why now, Sat?' she asked me. 'It's been more than two years . . .'

Amanda Ryan's bright blue eyes were studying my reaction, as if she was trying to catch me out. I wanted to look away but I couldn't. I was like a rabbit, watching the car approaching, blinded by the lights, knowing I was dead but accepting my fate.

'Because I need to talk,' I replied with a croak. Someone dropped a cup somewhere, and the coffee machine hissed as the waiter began to froth milk for a cappuccino.

'I appreciate that, Mr Kooner . . . but why tell me?' she said in her soft, melodic voice.

This time I had to look away. I thought back over the past four years, to the time when I was fifteen and life was so easy. I didn't have a care in the world then; didn't think

3

about anything. It was all about me and my shit: the girlfriend, the mates, football. I was so selfish, I didn't even think about her. Didn't listen when she spoke, or ask questions when she remained silent. Back then, all I wanted was to get away. Away from my family and their annoying traditions. Away from the feeling that I was being suffocated. I wanted to see things, be someone and live my life. Not once did I wonder if she wanted the same. If we were the same underneath.

'Have you told the police?' the journalist went on.

I shook my head.

'But I don't understand . . .' She was a picture of confusion. Her hair was tree-bark brown, her lips full and pink. Three small moles like dabs of chocolate paint worked diagonally across her left cheek.

'You helped Jennifer Barton write the story that first time,' I said.

Amanda half smiled. 'I was a young reporter then,' she explained. 'It was my first job. I'm not much further down the line now . . . And I don't know what I'm supposed to say.'

I shrugged. 'This is all of it,' I told her. 'Everything I know, from the beginning . . .'

She looked down at her notebook. The page was fresh and

4

empty of words, waiting for a story. She sighed. 'Look, I know it's been really hard and it must still hurt, but—'

'We know the truth now, all of us. That the Atwals probably killed my sister,' I said suddenly.

Her eyes lit up. 'I'm sorry?' she replied. 'Did you just say . . . ?'

I nodded.

'But the police followed the case until it was exhausted,' she said.

'Yeah, they did. Only there are things they don't know . . .'

She picked up her pen and tapped the end against her notebook. I watched her for a while, wondering whether I was doing the right thing. I'd helped to hide the truth. Only it was getting harder and harder to keep going. The guilt ate at my brain all day long, every day. The voice in my head was shouting. Most nights I woke up shivering, drenched in sweat, unable to shake her face from my mind.

'OK,' she said finally.

I thought about everything my family had faced. The threats and the danger. Then I thought about her, and my eyes began to well with tears. I gulped down air, tried to clear my thoughts. The coffee machine hissed on, customers chatted and gossiped, cups were set down on saucers, the door opened and closed with a ping, a chair was scraped across the floor, someone ripped open the cellophane around a piece of cake . . .

'Mr Kooner?'

'I've got evidence now, and a witness,' I revealed.

Amanda Ryan gasped. Her face fell but her eyes lit up.

'Can I tell you?'

She looked around, made sure no one was listening. 'Yes,' she replied. 'But not here. My flat is ten minutes away; what time do you have to be back in Leicester?'

I shrugged, realizing that there was no going back now. There was no way out. 'I don't . . .' I replied. 'At least, not for anything in particular. To be honest, I'd be better off staying in London for a while.'

She smiled, stood up and gathered her things. 'Come on,' she said.

ONE

It started when I was fifteen and living with my parents in a suburb called Oadby. My dad owned shops – a newsagent's, an off-licence and a chippy. We had a six-bedroomed house with a garden all the way round. I was the youngest of three. Amar, my brother, was twenty-four and married. He lived up the road, in a house that my dad had bought. His wife, Mandy, was pregnant with my nephew. My sister, Jas, was eighteen and recently married. She lived on the other side of Leicester, but it wasn't far. Nothing in Leicester is.

Amar was very business-minded and took after my old man. Both wore turbans and beards, but neither of them were proper Sikhs; they liked drinking too much. They were the same build too – short and stocky with hooked noses and big shoulders. My brother was like Dad's mini-me.

Jas was tall and slim. She had pale cream-coloured skin and deep brown eyes, the same colour as mine. She was so pretty that my mates all fancied her. Her hair was naturally light brown, and sometimes people thought she was mixed-race. One of our neighbours, a lovely old guy called Keith, teased her all the time. Told her that she was probably the milkman's daughter.

'If I was twenty years younger . . .' he'd say, leaning on his stick, before setting off up the road with his dog.

Jas didn't really notice the attention. At least, it came across that way. She was quiet and respectful – the 'perfect' Punjabi daughter. She never answered back to my parents, never rebelled against them. Sometimes she was like a ghost . . .

I was the youngest, the loudest and constantly in trouble. I didn't mean to cause trouble – it just happened. Like, if my dad wanted something done, Jas and Amar would do it straight away, no questions. Me, I would ask him why. It was the same with Mum. By the time I was fifteen they had pretty much given up trying to control me.

It's funny that I said *control*. When I think back, that is probably what it was, especially for my dad. He wasn't a tyrant or anything – he just wanted his kids to behave in a certain way. Loads of other dads were worse – men who were alcoholics or violent. My dad wasn't like that. He just had his ways, if that makes any sense.

Anyway, I was the one who had tantrums and played loud music. I hardly ever went to family functions or helped out in the shops. Instead, I'd disappear into town, play football or just hang out with my mates. At fourteen, I went to some boring family wedding, drank half a bottle of vodka and puked everywhere. I made a right twat of myself. However, despite their anger, my

8

parents were never violent or anything. They shouted, screamed, and banned me from going out, yeah. They never, ever hit any of us, though.

My family is massive. I have so many uncles, aunts and cousins that I can never remember all their names – not at the same time. Back then, we had masses of family functions. Every weekend there was a birthday or wedding; or some kind of blessing ceremony at the *gurdwara*, the Sikh temple. Not that most of my family were true Sikhs – they weren't. Most of the men were like Amar and Dad: they drank alcohol, ate meat, and a few smoked in secret. That's how things were. Not good, not bad – just normal.

My mum was the only practising Sikh in our house, the only regular at the *gurdwara*. I'd stopped going by the time I was twelve, although my mum still gave me grief. She spent years hounding Dad too, but it never worked. He would just smile, open a can of lager and scoff a bacon sandwich.

Mum was short, with long black hair and tiny hands and feet. She was overweight too because she loved all those Indian sweets – *jelebi*, *barfi*, *ladoo*, anything. That's where her diabetes came from. She was a happy person and didn't really work. Occasionally she'd go to one of the shops, but mostly she was at home, cooking our dinner or watching the telly.

The first argument I remember is a blur. It was about

six months after Jas's wedding – just after my fifteenth birthday in October – and Jas was staying at ours. She'd come for one night but my mum had convinced her to stay longer. She had lost some weight and looked ill. As soon as Mum mentioned it, though, I was out of the door, not interested. I went up to my room and started playing on my games console – one of those games where you shoot people and steal cars.

I'd been up there for twenty minutes when I heard their voices get louder. Jas was yelling at my mum, telling her that she didn't understand. My mum's voice was even louder, asking Jas to calm down and show respect. I went down to the living room, wondering what was going on.

'What's with the shouting?' I asked, looking at my sister. She'd never raised her voice before, not that I knew of, and I was a bit shocked. Only she didn't look angry or anything. She just looked sad.

'It's nothing,' replied Mum. 'We were talking about someone . . .'

'Who?' I asked.

'No one you know, *beteh*. Go and do something else – I want to talk to your sister.'

I shrugged, got a drink from the kitchen and returned to my room. Even though it was strange to hear Jas raising her voice, I soon forgot all about it. She was an adult and she was married. To be honest, I was pleased to see her standing up for herself for once . . .

Neither Jas nor Amar *chose* to get married. They didn't go out with people or have dates – nothing like that. My family did all the matchmaking. Amar was nineteen when he got sorted. Most of his close friends were Punjabi like us, and they were all married too, or thinking about it. Amar met a few girls over the summer, round at one of my uncles'. Before I could blink, he'd said yes to one of them and that was that. His wife, Mandeep, came from Birmingham, and she was pretty and friendly. She had that funny Brummie accent too, and I used to enjoy taking the piss. The way they'd met seemed strange to me, but they came across as happy enough.

It was different for Jas, though – she *had* to get married. She'd been going to a local college, training to be a beautician and enjoying it. Then everything got messed up. Some old gossip who lived up the road told my dad that Jas had a boyfriend; an Asian lad who went to her college. When Dad asked her, Jas went bright red and denied it. Only he didn't believe her. He got angry and called her names. He said that she'd dishonoured him, ruined his good name. My sister never admitted that the accusation was true, but she still paid the price.

My parents pulled Jas out of college, and within

two months she'd been fixed up with some man. I remember thinking she'd gone mental. She wasn't angry or upset or anything. She acted like it was nothing.

'*Were* you going out with him?' I asked her eventually when we were sitting together in the conservatory.

'No, Sat,' she replied. 'It was just some lad . . .'

'But aren't you angry with that woman?'

Jas shrugged. 'Not really – it was a mistake. She didn't mean any harm.'

'But look what happened!' I said. 'They stopped you going to college and everything. I'd go mental . . .'

'Mum and Dad only want what's best for us,' she told me. 'I can always do *another* course after I'm married. I *can't* get another mum and dad.'

I didn't understand her, though. There's no way I'd let Dad run *my* life; but Jas was different. She just seemed to accept things. It makes her sound strange, but she wasn't. She was just . . . Jas.

'So who you getting married to?'

'I dunno much about him,' she admitted. 'We only met last week. He seems OK . . .'

'Just OK?'

She gave me a funny look. 'His name's Taswinder Atwal.'

'When's the wedding?'

'Next summer,' she replied, switching TV channels

and ending the conversation.

The argument between Mum and Jas continued until my dad came home from work. Then it stopped. Jas came up and asked me what I wanted to eat.

'Dunno,' I replied. 'What's Mum made?'

'*Dal, roti* . . .'

'Stuff that,' I said, pulling a face. 'I'm gonna get a kebab.'

'What you up to?' she asked, looking around my room.

I followed her eyes and felt ashamed. My clothes were scattered across the floor. Textbooks and projects cluttered my desk, burying my laptop. The shelves were overflowing with books, old toys and all sorts of other crap. Peeping out from under my bed was a copy of *Nuts* magazine. I edged over to it, praying that my sister hadn't seen the naked blonde woman on the cover. I kicked it under the bed.

'Smells in here,' she said, half smiling. Back then, I didn't notice how tired she looked. I wish I had.

'Smells like your pants,' I joked, like I'd done as a kid.

'More like your bum!' she added, joining in.

'You wanna kebab?' I asked her.

'Yeah . . . come on – I'll drive you. Taz got me a car. BMW one-one-eight.'

I whistled. 'Taz is proper rich, i'n't he?' I said.

Jas nodded.

'You're well lucky!'

If I *had* been paying attention, I would have seen it. The distant look in her eyes, the slight shadow that fell across her face. If I could go back . . .

TWO

Two days after that first argument, I was getting my lunch when Taz drove by. He was in a blue Jaguar XKR – a five-litre supercharged V8 with over 500 horsepower, my mate Dash explained.

'And that colour, bro – *kyanite* blue, exclusive to that car,' he said. Dash was obsessed with cars; he could tell you everything about any car you cared to mention. Even stuff you didn't want to know.

If Taz saw me, he didn't show it. We were standing outside Greggs in Oadby when he went by, disappearing round the bend. He had two passengers with him: big, heavy-set men with shaven heads.

'Best get back to class,' I said.

'What's he do for a living?' asked Dash.

'Just stuff with bars and that,' I replied.

Taz owned two bars and a club, and did promotions for Asian music shows. His dad owned loads of property – which is where Taz's money came from – but he was in prison now. Even so, my dad was proud that Taz had agreed to marry Jas.

'Millionaires,' he'd told me at the time, smiling and taking a big glug of Chivas Regal. 'We must have impressed them.'

I bit into the sausage roll I'd bought for lunch. It was straight out of the oven and set my mouth on fire. *'OWW!'*

Bits of pastry and pig flew out of my mouth, just as two girls from school walked past.

'You're nasty,' said Charlotte, a white girl with dark hair and serious good looks. I'd fancied her for ages. Her mate, Pooja, was Asian with blonde highlights and green eyes.

'Sat's been nasty since we went to Brookside,' said Pooja – Brookside was our junior school.

They giggled and went into Greggs. An old Asian woman walked past, saw the sausage roll on the pavement and cussed me.

'Charlotte looked well impressed,' teased Dash.

'Piss off!'

We made it back just in time. I went into English, brushing the crumbs off my jacket.

The teacher, Miss Woodward, winked at me. 'Those sausage rolls can be a killer,' she said with a smile.

I looked over at Charlotte and Pooja, who started laughing. Eventually Miss Woodward began her lesson on *Lord of the Flies*.

'So what's the importance of the shell that the boys find?' she asked the class.

When Pooja put up her hand, some of the lads sniggered; the stupid ones who talked like gangsters.

They were all rich kids who'd shit their pants if they saw a real rudeboy. There were loads of them where I lived.

'It's a symbol of authority, miss,' said Pooja.

Charlotte was listening with her head propped on her hand. Her wavy hair was the colour of melted milk chocolate, cut just below her jaw line. Her caramel-coloured eyes shone. I wondered what her skin smelled like. Daydreamed about kissing her.

'. . . Ralph and Piggy?' said Miss Woodward, finishing a question.

Suddenly everyone was looking at me.

'What?' I asked.

'More attention to what I'm saying, Sat. You can gaze at Charlotte later,' Miss Woodward told me.

Some of the pupils whistled and cheered, but Miss Woodward repeated her question. I noticed that Charlotte was looking at me and thought hard and fast. Recalling something I'd read on the BBC revision site, I managed to answer the question. Miss Woodward nodded and gave me a big smile.

'Well done, Sat – that's exactly what I was looking for,' she said.

I looked over at Charlotte and grinned. She smiled back and I nearly fell off my chair.

Jas's mother-in-law came round that night. Taz's older

brother, Ricky, was with her. He was stocky and well muscled, with a shaved head. He wore an expensive-looking light grey suit over a lilac shirt and silvery tie. I'd seen him at the wedding and knew him to talk to. Amar and Mandy were there too, sitting with my parents.

I found my sister in the kitchen, making tea. She was wearing a traditional Punjabi outfit and loads of matching red and gold bangles on her wrists.

'What's with the decorations?' I asked. 'You look like a Christmas tree.'

'They're called *chura*,' she explained. 'You get them on your wedding day. You have to wear them to show you're recently married.'

'Why?' I asked, looking at my mum's special tea set – the one she kept for important guests – which sat on the worktop.

'Why what?' said Jas.

'Why do you *have* to wear them?'

She shook her head. 'You don't know much, do you? It's called tradition.'

'Bullshit, more like,' I said, grinning.

'Just get some biscuits out, will you?' she said, looking flustered.

'You going back then?' I continued, getting the biscuits out of the cupboard.

My sister's one-night stay had lasted a week. Not

18

that it was a big deal; it was nice to have her around – I'd missed her.

'I don't know . . .' She didn't meet my eyes.

'Don't you miss Taz?'

Jas was making Indian-style tea. She'd boiled water and milk together with the tea bags in a saucepan. She turned down the heat and started to set the china cups and sugar bowl out on a tray.

'It's not about missing him,' she replied, not making any sense.

I gave her a look, which she didn't see.

'But—' I began.

'Our marriage was arranged,' she reminded me. 'It's about duty, not love. That's for *other* people . . .'

I didn't understand what she was saying so I changed the subject.

'Is Taz coming?'

'I don't think so – he's just gone to Spain on business.'

'*Yeah?*' I asked, trying to imagine myself being *that* successful. Travelling to other countries and running a big business of my own.

Jas looked straight at me. 'He goes away all the time.'

I nodded and put some expensive M&S biscuits onto a plate.

'I've got samosas in the oven,' she said. 'Could you put them out too?'

I grabbed a white chocolate-covered biscuit and stuffed it into my gob. 'Just checking they're OK,' I joked when I'd swallowed it. 'Don't wanna kill the in-laws.'

Jas shook her head and smiled a little.

I sat with the adults for twenty minutes, being polite. I knew that Dad would bang on at me otherwise – and besides, I needed cash. Pissing him off, then asking for hundred-quid Timberlands would be a stupid move. I spent the time chatting to Ricky about football and stuff.

'You should come down the Dice bar,' he suggested.

'Ain't old enough,' I reminded him.

He ruffled my hair. 'No age restrictions on family,' he told me. 'When my brother took your sister on, he got you lot too – that's how us Punjabis run our shit.'

I nodded.

'Besides,' Ricky continued, 'you don't look young. Just dress up smart and I'll sort you out.'

'Serious?' I asked.

'Yeah . . . I'll leave you my number – Taz's too. Anytime you're out, call me and I'll hook you up, little bro.'

Eventually my dad offered Ricky a shot of Chivas. He refused a few times before Amar poured him a large one anyway. I could tell that Ricky had only refused out

20

of politeness. It was a real Asian thing – saying no to be polite, and then having a drink anyway. They did it over booze, presents, money – all kinds of shit. It made me laugh.

I left them to it and watched telly in the conservatory. Not before reminding Ricky to leave his number, though.

'Don't worry,' he said. 'Even if I forget, Jas has got it.'

'Nice one.'

THREE

The following week Pooja started following me around school, asking me questions. What music I liked and what TV shows I watched – all sorts. She even wanted to know whether I preferred plain or patterned boxer shorts, which was the most random of the lot. Like that would make any difference to anyone. Eventually she told me that Charlotte liked me.

'You should ask her out – go and see a film or something,' she suggested.

'Yeah,' I replied. '*If* you ain't winding me up.'

Pooja flicked her blonde highlights and pulled a face. 'Why would I do that?'

'Because you wanna take the piss.'

'You're paranoid,' she said, grinning like a nutter.

'Why *you* askin' me?' I asked her. 'Why not Charlotte?'

'Ain't very romantic, is it?' Pooja replied. 'Like she's gonna come beg you for a date? Most lads would form a queue . . .'

'So I've gotta beg now, yeah?' I said jokingly.

Pooja nodded. 'My friend is a goddess. Bow down at her feet and take your reward, Satinder Kooner.'

I grinned at the way she'd used my full name. No one called me that – not even my parents, unless they were angry with me. 'You're a proper loony,' I told her.

'Might be,' she said, grinning again. 'But I'm a loony with a *buff* best friend, so you'd better start being nice to me.'

That's how it happened. Ten minutes later, I saw Charlotte in the kiosk queue at Sainsbury's, getting her lunch. I went over and used the 'let's go see a film' suggestion from Pooja. Charlotte went a bit red, smiled and gave me her number.

'Call me tonight,' she said. She looked gorgeous: she'd tied up her hair and wore a light blue dress that buttoned down the front, over a white, three-quarter sleeve top and indigo jeans with Converse boots. She smelled of vanilla.

I smiled back at her. 'OK,' I replied, noticing two wannabe-gangsters giving me a stare.

Every man at school wanted to get with Charlotte. I was going to get plenty of dirty looks. *Bring it*, I thought as I went back to join Dash.

'Sorted?' he asked me.

'The girl is mine,' I said proudly.

'You lucky bastard,' replied Dash, turning back to the sandwich fridge. 'Who puts tandoori chicken in a sandwich, bro? With *yoghurt*! That's just nasty.'

My parents never asked me about my social life and I never told them. I was happy that way too. They were old-fashioned Punjabi, so girlfriends were out. It was disrespectful, to their way of thinking. If I wanted a woman, I was supposed to ask them to find me a wife; arrange it all for me. Only that wasn't happening. I wasn't getting married young, not like Amar and Jas. I wanted to enjoy myself. I never told them about Charlotte and she didn't seem to care, anyway.

'None of my business,' she'd said when I explained my parents' backward ways.

'Yeah, but don't think I'm ashamed of you or anything,' I'd told her.

'I won't, Sat – not unless you make me.'

I was out all the time, mostly with Charlotte. If she was busy, I'd go see Dash or some other mates. I never stayed in. Whether I was hanging out at Charlotte's house, listening to music in her bedroom and doing them things you do, or hanging around on the streets with Dash and the others, something was always going on. I played football on Tuesdays and Thursdays, and went round to Dash's house most Wednesdays to kick ass on his PlayStation.

My parents, apart from the usual shit, didn't really try to stop me. Occasionally my dad would bang on about working in the chippy or the off-licence, but I never did. I used homework, projects or football as an excuse. That year, after Jas got married, I grew further and further away from my family. Not because I didn't love them. I just missed what was going on because I was never there. I didn't know what they were doing. And I didn't really care.

By New Year's Eve my relationship with Charlotte was going strong. I decided to take up Ricky's offer and got some tickets for Dice bar. I had to lie to my dad, though. He didn't want me to go out, but when I mentioned Taz and Ricky, his attitude changed. *Respect* and *honour* were big things to Dad. As the family of the bride, we had to show respect to the Atwals. They had taken the *burden* of a daughter from my parents, and we were supposed to be grateful. It was all bullshit to me, but my dad swore by the old traditions. Whatever he did, he did by the rules. So when I told him that Taz had invited me, he actually started smiling.

'You should have said so, *beteh*,' he said.

'I can't let them down,' I added, pushing my luck.

'No. Take some money before you go. Don't let them think we have empty pockets.'

Dad told me to listen to everything Taz said. To respect him. 'My *izzat* is at stake,' he went on, not making any sense. What did going out for a beer with Taz and my dad's *honour* have in common?

'Don't worry, Dad,' I replied. 'I won't disgrace you.'

It was snowing when we got to Dice, and the city centre

was busy with people. The queue was massive. I had four tickets – one each for me, Charlotte, Pooja and Dash. I looked at the crowd waiting to get in, huddling together to stay warm.

'Ricky said to join the VIP,' I told Charlotte. She was wearing a short black dress and high heels. The skin on her arms was red because of the cold.

'Hurry up then,' she replied, putting her arms around me. 'It's freezing out here.'

'Should have worn a jacket,' I teased her.

'What?' she asked, her eyes sparkling. 'Don't I look good?'

I nodded. 'You look amazing.' I wondered what she thought of my clothes. I was wearing a pair of dark jeans with a white shirt, maroon sweater and navy pinstriped jacket. I'd also borrowed some brown Chelsea boots from Amar.

We walked up to the door, ignoring the dirty looks we were getting. Someone swore at us. I began to worry about getting in. Despite what Ricky had said, I felt like a little kid, dressed up for no reason. The bouncers would know we were underage. We saw that there was a smaller queue to the right of the door. A tall woman in a black puffa jacket, dark blue jeans and bright white trainers was standing by it, holding a clipboard.

'This is the guest list queue,' she said, giving me a big smile, 'and I can't see any school outings on it.'

My heart sank and Charlotte pinched my side.

'I thought you said it was sorted,' she said. She didn't seem angry or pissed off. If anything, she looked amused. She was like that: things didn't really bother her too much.

'Er . . .' I began, seeing Dash pull a face. 'Ricky put us down . . .'

The woman with the clipboard looked down the list, frowning. 'Ricky?'

'Yeah,' I told her. 'I'm Taz Atwal's brother-in-law.'

'Wait here . . .' She shrugged at a huge bouncer with massive shoulders wearing a long black coat. His freshly shaved head looked red and sore. He walked across, took the clipboard from the woman, and gave us a funny look.

'You reckon Ricky and Taz put you down?' he asked. His eyes were pale blue and cold. He didn't blink once.

I nodded.

'Name?'

'Sat Kooner,' I replied. 'There's four of us.'

The doorman nodded. 'You're on the list,' he said, looking surprised.

'I know,' I told him. 'Ricky and Taz are family.'

The doorman smiled at me. 'One of them *Asian* things, is it?' He still hadn't blinked. He was grinning at me but his eyes were dead.

'What do you mean?' I asked him, looking away.

28

'I get about fifty people every week – claiming to be family.'

I shrugged. 'Ask Ricky,' I replied. I was annoyed, but I tried not to show it. Winding up a bouncer would only cause trouble.

'Nice girl you've got there,' he said. Another smirk that failed to reach his eyes. 'Does she give it some . . . ?'

I turned away when he winked, anger flaring inside me.

When Laura walked in, Taz Atwal was sitting in the office looking at the sales figures from the previous week. Money — small amounts of it — had been going missing for a while. A hundred short here, fifty quid there. He was trying to spot a pattern, but instead of finding one, he had given himself a headache.

'Got some lad outside — looks about sixteen,' Laura told him.

Taz took a sip of his Jack Daniel's and Coke, the glass sweating in the heat of the small room, and shrugged. 'So tell him to do one.' He wondered why she was bothering him with something he paid her to sort out.

'He says that Ricky put him on the list . . .'

Taz turned to his older brother, who was sitting at his desk, texting someone. 'You been putting kids on the guest list, bro?'

Ricky shook his head. In front of him, on an empty CD case, were neat little lines of yellowy-white powder and a small barber's blade. There were eight lines, none longer than an inch. 'I don't know any kids,' he replied.

Laura sighed. She had grown tired of working at Dice.

Taz and Ricky were always getting things mixed up. One would put names on the guest list — only for the other to cross them off again. Or they'd argue about the way the bar was arranged. Ricky spent most of his time shagging bar staff or off his head, not leaving until the cleaners arrived first thing in the morning. He'd nearly set fire to the place twice, passing out with a fag in his hand. There were better ways of making a living. Only Taz wouldn't approve . . .

'He says he's your brother-in-law,' said Laura.

'I ain't got a brother-in-law,' replied Ricky, leaning across the CD cover with a rolled-up £20 note.

'Your brother-in-law,' explained Laura, looking at Taz.

'Bollocks . . . What's that dickhead doing here?' Taz was pissed off.

Ricky looked up. A smudge of cocaine powder sat on his top lip. 'Shit,' he said, sniffing hard and wiping his nose. 'Yeah — I put him down.'

Laura looked at Taz and shook her head. 'He's underage.'

'No big deal,' replied Ricky. 'Besides, he's family.'

'Taz?' asked Laura.

Taz turned to his brother, who was now lighting a cigarette. 'What you playin' at?'

'Nuttin',' said Ricky, blowing out smoke. 'When I took

32

Mum round that time, I said he could come down. He don't look that young.'

'Yeah, but why? I don't want anyone sneaking around here.'

Ricky grinned. 'What's he gonna see, Taz? He'll get pissed and go home, like the rest of the punters. What's the big deal?'

'What shall I do?' Laura asked impatiently.

'Let him in,' said Taz. 'But if he asks, I'm busy.'

'And get him a free round too,' added Ricky, with a big grin. 'Family and all that . . .'

When Laura had gone, Taz turned to his brother. 'You off your head or what?' he asked, walking over to his desk.

Ricky gestured towards the cocaine. 'I'm trying to get that way,' he joked.

'Like I give a fuck about that little shit or his family . . .' Taz continued.

'Appearances . . .' said Ricky, reminding him of something they'd discussed when he'd married Jas. 'Do what you like, bro, but keep up appearances.'

'You don't,' said Taz. 'You ain't stuck with some bitch because the family want it . . .'

Ricky shrugged. 'Been there, done that. Best not go there again, hey bro?'

Taz thought about the two years that Ricky had been married and the way it had ended. 'Yeah, probably best not to . . .'

'Just suck it up, bro.' Ricky offered Taz the rolled-up note. 'Ain't like it really affects you anyway. You still got Laura – not to mention them other slappers.'

Taz took the note and grinned. 'True,' he said, taking another sip of his drink.

'And when you *do* go home, you've got a nice fresh Indian takeaway to keep you sweet too. I wouldn't be complaining . . .'

FOUR

The doorman was gutted. He shrugged, gave me an evil look.

'I'll be responsible if anything happens,' the woman told him.

He nodded. 'Too right,' he told her. 'I ain't losing my door licence because Taz don't know how to say no.'

'Yeah, right . . .' The woman shook her head. 'Which licence? Who are you this week – Tommy or Fred?'

He glared at her. 'Loose lips . . .' he said in an angry whisper. 'Just shut up, Laura, and do your job.'

Laura looked at Charlotte and me. 'One free drink each.' She handed Charlotte a load of vouchers. 'Have a good night.'

I led the way in; behind me, Dash and Pooja were starting to get excited.

'I felt like a kid, standing there,' said Pooja. 'I was ready to go home.'

Dash grinned at her and whispered, 'We *are* kids.'

'*You* might be,' Pooja told him, smoothing down her red dress. 'Me, I'm a young *adult*.'

It was obvious that we were underage. As we made for the bar, through a thick crowd, a few people stared at us. Most of the revellers looked much older and I felt self-conscious. A blonde woman with skin like an orange joked that she'd taught me to read. Her tiny yellow dress barely held her boobs in.

'They'll get bored in a minute,' Charlotte told me when I complained. 'Besides – she looks like a poster girl for Slappers dot com.'

'Guess so.' I looked around. 'Wonder where they are?'

'Who?'

'Taz and Ricky,' I replied, ignoring Dash and Pooja, who were still dissing each other.

'Dunno about them,' said Charlotte with a grin, 'but I think love is in the air.'

She nodded towards Dash, who was grinning like a moron, trying to come up with clever lines to use on Pooja. Only Pooja was too sharp for him.

'There's a sale on at Asda,' she told him. 'Training pants are half price – Pampers pull-ups.'

'I prefer buy-one-get-one-free,' said Dash, like a fool.

'Er . . .' replied Pooja, 'I think you'll find that half price is the same as BOGOF.'

'Eh?' Dash looked confused.

'BOGOF,' repeated Pooja. 'Buy-one-get-one-free – same as half price.'

'Why are you talking about supermarkets?' countered Dash.

Pooja smiled. Like a hyena with a dead antelope at its feet. 'Just preparing you for your future career.'

When we finally reached the bar, Dash and Pooja took a break from each other and ordered drinks: two each because the bar was so busy. I took hold of Charlotte. Her dress tied across the shoulders and around the neck, exposing her back. Her skin had warmed up; it was smooth and soft.

'You marking your territory?' she asked me.

'What?'

'Putting your hand on me – warning other blokes off?'

I smiled and took my hand away.

'I didn't say stop,' she said, putting it back. I leaned in and kissed her. The scent on her skin was amazing – warm and spicy.

'Can't help it,' I told her. 'You're stunning.'

She grinned at me and moved closer. I could feel every curve of her body against mine.

'Ooh!' she giggled. 'You've got my New Year's present in your pocket.'

I felt myself go red. 'Er . . .' I began.

She shut me up with a kiss.

We stood at the back, close to the bar and the DJ, laughing as Pooja and Dash flirted with each other. One minute they'd be arguing; the next, dancing close together, grinning like idiots. By midnight we were in a great mood. Not too pissed or anything – just really happy and chilled. Then, just after the turn of the year, Charlotte asked me where my sister was.

'Don't you want to give her a hug or something?' she asked me.

'My sister?'

Charlotte nodded. 'I want to meet her,' she added.

I shook my head. 'She won't be here.'

Charlotte gave me a funny look. 'But this is Taz's bar,' she pointed out, 'and she's his wife. Why wouldn't she be here?'

I wondered how to explain the differences between my family and Charlotte's. It was weird because, although we were both British, Charlotte came from one culture and I was from another. We were like the same, and then different too. It wasn't easy to explain.

'It's not like that for Jas,' I told her. 'She's quite traditional . . .'

'But Taz is *here*.' Charlotte looked confused.

'This is where he *works*,' I explained. 'It's not like having fun – it's just what he does.'

She frowned. 'If I was Jas, *I'd* be out, especially if my husband owned the place.'

'Jas doesn't really go out,' I replied. 'She never has.'

'Oh,' said Charlotte, looking disappointed. 'I was hoping to say hello . . .'

38

'You can,' I told her. 'I'll sort something out.'

'So she's just at home – doing nothing?'

I shrugged. 'She might be round at mine.'

Charlotte frowned again. 'You're just *weird*,' she told me. 'Not knowing what your family are doing on New Year's?'

'No big deal,' I said.

Charlotte hiccupped and moved closer. 'You haven't touched my bum for ages,' she whispered into my ear, changing the subject.

'*And* . . . ?'

'And I think you should,' she said, swaying a bit. 'It's *very* nice . . .'

She turned round, rubbing her bum against me. I tried to ignore the sensation but it was no use. The more excited I got, the more Charlotte teased me. I put my hands around her waist and kissed the back of her neck. She turned round again, took my left hand and placed it on a breast.

'I really, really like you,' she said, her pale brown eyes sparkling.

'I like you too,' I replied.

'How much?'

I smiled, pulled her towards me and kissed her.

We left half an hour later, hoping to get a cab home. The snow had stopped falling but covered the ground, inches deep. The street outside Dice was full of people shaking, shivering, and falling about. My teeth chattered because I'd let Charlotte have my jacket.

'Waiting for the school bus?'

I turned and saw the big doorman. He was grinning at me.

'Piss off,' I replied, the booze making me brave and stupid.

'Take the goods home, little man,' he said. 'I'm here most days – if you fancy getting your face torn off.'

'Yeah?' I asked.

'Paki wanker . . .' he muttered.

'You what?'

'Oh, nothing. Off you go now . . .'

I'd heard him, and so had Dash.

'You wanna call Taz and tell him,' he muttered to me. Pooja nuzzled her head into his chest. She was *at least* as pissed as Charlotte.

I thought about what Dash had said, and nodded. 'Yeah . . .'

I called Ricky because I didn't have Taz's number. He answered on the third ring.

'You havin' a good night?' I heard him shout over the noise of the bar.

'Can I talk to you?' I asked.

'Wait,' he replied. 'Can't hear jack . . .'

I heard the music receding as he found a quieter spot.

Eventually he spoke again.

'What was that, Sat?'

I told him that we were outside, looking for a cab and getting abuse from his doorman.

'*That* prick?' he said, with a chuckle. 'He don't mean nothing by it – ignore him.'

'I would,' I replied, 'if we could find a taxi.'

'Tell you what,' said Ricky, 'I need to pick up some mates. Gimme a minute and I'll come out and give you a lift.'

'Really?' I asked, smiling to myself.

'No problem.'

I heard raised voices, male and female. Taz was nearby, giving one of his staff a bollocking. I ignored it and thanked Ricky.

'One minute,' he said before hanging up.

I turned to Dash. 'Ricky's on his way out,' I told him.

'To sort that ape on the door?' he asked.

I shook my head. 'Even better. He's gonna drop us off.'

A few moments later Ricky joined us. He spoke to the bouncer and they had a laugh. Then he turned to me.

'He apologizes for any offence,' he said. 'He's got them anger-management issues . . .'

'More like dick-for-a-head issues,' I said, feeling better.

Ricky looked the girls up and down. 'You two got some *taste* in women,' he said, grinning.

He unlocked the blue Jaguar XKR that I'd seen Taz driving. 'Come on – get in.'

'*This* is a motor,' gasped Dash.

Ricky ruffled my hair, making me feel like a five-year-old. I didn't say anything, though – not when he'd been so nice to us.

'You enjoy yourself?' he asked.

'Yeah, Ricky. Thanks for the tickets . . .'

He winked at me, looked at Charlotte, and then winked again.

It's her first night in the marital bed and he's turned up drunk. She's spent the last few hours listening to guidance from his mother and sisters. And from a few aunts too; thick-set, overweight women caked in make-up, saturated in perfume. She's been fed, watered, and shown where to put her clothes. She's been anointed and blessed. Then, just in case she hasn't understood, she's been given yet more advice. He is a good boy, a sensible boy. However, he has his ways: the drinking and staying out all night. Not because he is a bad boy; no, not that. Just like his father, he is misunderstood. It's just his business, one that has made him rich. She would rather he stayed out all night and came home with money, she is told, than sit around wasting his life like some little man with no ambition.

She'd have preferred to be left alone, but that won't happen any more. Her life is going to become one long family event. No more time to herself, no more chances to be herself. She's going to become theirs: *their* daughter, *his* wife, *her* sister-in-law. They are going to own her life, own her belongings, own her . . .

He asks her if she is OK, and she nods. He goes into the en-suite shower room and takes off his expensive hand-stitched and tailored suit. Washes then dries himself with a soft towel of cream Egyptian cotton; uses the loo. When he returns to her, he wears nothing except his boxer shorts, tight and white, and a smile. She doesn't see that it's a drunken, drugged-up smile. That will come later, when she learns the truth about his ways. For now, he is the doting new husband . . .

Ten minutes later, he's pulling on jeans and a white shirt with old trainers. There are still guests around, he tells her. He has to go and see them. The lads are waiting too, and he can't let the lads down. She tells him she doesn't mind. And she doesn't. As he leaves her, she tries to ignore the fact that her skin now reeks of alcohol. She tries to dismiss the taste of tobacco and mint that he has deposited in her mouth with his saliva. She gets up, opens a window, then walks slowly to the shower room. She glances down at herself, her full breasts and long legs. Something churns in her belly; acidic bile rises up into her mouth.

FIVE

I had more than a hangover on New Year's Day. My head was thumping and my nose was running. My throat felt sandpapered. I lay in my bed, trying to swallow and not puke. Eventually I cleaned my teeth, thinking it would help, but the toothbrush made me gag. I was shivering too, which could only mean one thing: I had the flu. Back in my room, I lay down and groaned, cursing the shitty start to my New Year.

I awoke with a start about an hour later. A door slammed shut and I heard loud voices. I got up and looked out across the U-shaped landing. My mum was at Jas's bedroom door. My sister must have spent the night here.

'What's up?' I asked.

'It's nothing,' Mum replied. 'It's nearly lunch time and you're still sleeping.'

She said the last part as a statement. She always did that whenever I slept in, which was all the time. To be honest, even without the flu, I would have stayed in bed. There was nothing else to do on New Year's morning.

'I've got the flu,' I told her.

My mum looked concerned. 'Go and make some Lemsip.'

'I'll have a shower first,' I replied.

'If you're going to stay out until all hours . . .'

'Yeah,' I said, shutting the door.

When I got downstairs, my dad was in the conservatory watching some old film.

'Good morning,' he said, trying to be funny.

'I'm not well,' I said, sitting down and shivering some more.

'How was your night with Taswinder?' he asked.

That threw me for a moment. In my head was an image of Charlotte, leaning into my chest, smelling of spices, as I wrapped my arms around her.

'It was good,' I said, not looking at him.

'You didn't embarrass us, did you?'

'No,' I replied quickly. 'We had a few drinks and then I went off with my mates. Taz had business to see to.'

Dad gave me a funny look. 'Mates . . . ? Which mates?'

'Dash,' I replied. 'Him and some other lads from college.'

'They were out too?'

'Er . . . yeah. We all went together, and that.'

My dad's suspicions began to grow. I could see it in his face.

'But you said it was just you and Taswinder,' he said.

I bought time by finding a tissue and blowing my nose.

'It was. Taz wanted Dash to go too, though. He was busy running the bar, so I would have been on my own,' I lied.

Dad seemed happy with that and changed the subject. 'Honey and lemon and hot tea,' he said. 'Shot of brandy will help too.'

I grinned at him. 'Alcohol helps everything, according to you.'

He laughed. 'It's true. It is nature's medicine. Come on.'

We went into the kitchen together and found my brother and Mandy sitting at the table.

'You look terrible, Sat,' she said.

I shrugged. 'I've caught something, Mandy . . . Flu or summat . . .'

I looked at her rounded belly and started to worry. She must have seen me do it.

'Being pregnant doesn't mean I have to avoid all germs,' she said with a smile. 'But it's nice of you to consider me.'

I smiled, feeling a bit foolish. 'I just thought—'

'Sit down and shut up,' Mandy told me. 'I'll make you some Lemsip.'

My dad shook his head. 'Lemsip?' he snorted. 'That's rubbish. I'll show you a hot toddy. It's my own recipe – much better than Lemsip.'

Mandy gave my brother a look, but Amar just shrugged and adjusted his pale blue turban.

'They work for me,' he said.

'You mean the booze works.' She pulled a face. I couldn't tell if she was joking or being serious.

My brother pulled a face too.

'How come you're here?' I asked them.

'We're having lunch together,' replied Mandy.

'Indian or English?' I asked, hoping for the latter. The only day we *didn't* eat Indian food was Christmas. It was getting boring.

'A bit of both,' said Mandy. 'We got guests coming over.'

I raised my eyebrows. Relatives were about as welcome as a punch in the head. I wanted my bed.

'The Atwals,' she added.

'Cool,' I replied.

My phone began to vibrate in my pocket. I had three text messages. The first was Dash, banging on about the night before. The second was one of those New Year greetings from some random cousin. I ignored both. The final text was from Charlotte, thanking me for a great night. She was home alone and wanted me to join her. I texted back, telling her about the guests. I said I'd come round later, even though I was feeling like shit. Only Charlotte was ill too, according to her reply, but she didn't tell me to stay away.

'Who's that?' asked Mandy with a smile. 'Some girl?'

I shook my head. 'Two girls . . .' I joked. 'I'm in demand.'

The phone buzzed in my hand. It was Charlotte again, saying that she'd be waiting. I sent back a winking smiley as Dad handed me a steaming glass of nasty-looking liquid.

'Drink,' he told me. 'You'll be fine after that.'

'It looks radioactive,' I complained.

'It is,' Mandy said. 'You didn't see how much brandy went in.'

I looked at my dad, shrugged and downed half the glass. It was strong and bitter but felt good as it worked its way down my throat.

'Lovely,' said Dad before heading back to the conservatory.

Jas's new family turned up around three p.m. Her mother-in-law was first through the door, followed by an older man with a bald, shiny head and big square glasses. Behind him were two other women and then Taz. He looked annoyed and his face was almost grey. His eyes were red and ringed with dark circles.

'You look worse than me,' I joked.

'What?'

'After last night,' I added as he shook hands with Amar.

'Oh yeah,' he said, turning to me. 'Didn't get in until seven a.m.'

No wonder he looked so bad. I wondered why he'd

been so late when the bar had closed at three. He must have read my mind.

'Once the punters go home, we get to relax,' he explained. 'We took the staff to a late bar down by Braunstone Gate . . . Had a few too many,' he added.

I nodded as we went into the living room. 'Guess you've come to get Jas,' I said.

'Yeah,' he replied as he took a seat.

Dad told me to go and help my sister. I found her in the kitchen.

'You been hiding?' I asked.

'No,' she said quickly.

'What was all that shit this morning?'

She didn't look at me when she replied. 'It's private,' she said, pouring out the tea, 'and it was nearly the afternoon.'

'Suit yourself,' I told her. 'I was only asking.'

It's funny how you don't notice things sometimes – not even those that are right under your nose. I was so caught up in my own life that I didn't see any of the signs. Like the way Taz didn't seem to give a shit when I mentioned Jas. The way his eyes looked – the pupils nothing more than tiny black pinpricks. The tiredness in my sister's voice and the way she was pouring the tea, splashing it everywhere and not caring. The real Jas would have cleaned up the spillage immediately. It was a sign, just like the messy hair and the lack of make-up. I just didn't see it. I didn't care enough to see it.

By five p.m., despite my illness, I was out of the door, almost running to Charlotte's house. I had no idea that the next time I saw my sister's beautiful face, it would be the last.

SIX

That January was a mess, with heavy snow across the country. The Met Office had predicted an 'Arctic snap', but no one believed them. When the cold hit, there was chaos. Round our way, the schools stayed shut and people couldn't get to work. Every day for a week cars skidded and crashed on our road. The news was full of stories about things running out: it started with grit for the roads, but then it was gas and food too. I remember being in Sainsbury's with Dash and seeing a newspaper headline about empty supermarkets. All we could see was packed shelves.

'How can they just lie to people like that?' Dash asked me.

I remember wondering the same thing. If they could lie so blatantly about something that was so easy to check, why would we believe anything else they said?

Our school reopened just in time for the weekend, which seemed a bit stupid to me, but I guess it was important. There were mock exams coming up for our GCSEs, and for the sixth form too. I wasn't feeling any pressure, though. Exams were a challenge in the same way that a PlayStation game is. I was good at both and wouldn't let anyone beat me. I actually *enjoyed* taking tests. I did nothing all year, and then passed my exams easily, annoying the hell out of Dash.

The thing is, I *did* work. I read all the time and enjoyed learning new things. I just kept it hidden. At my school, if you were clever, you pretended you weren't. Otherwise you'd be called a geek. Most of the lads I knew put on a front; and for a long time that included me too. Hanging around outside the chippy or the off-licence and pretending to be bad boys, or giving the teachers backchat, trying to fit in with everyone else. Even though I joined in, I *knew* it was the geeks who'd be successful, so I was being a hypocrite. I wanted to be successful too. The *I'm not clever, honest* stuff was just an act. A blag.

Then it snowed again, only twice as hard, and the school had to close because the heating system broke down. I spent another four days doing nothing but slip and slide my way to Charlotte's house. While I was doing all that, things with Jas got worse and I never saw it coming. Maybe if someone had taped it to Charlotte's bra I would have noticed. Or if they'd published it on Google or Facebook. But that didn't happen.

Jas turned up on a Saturday when I was home alone. Looking back, it's easy to see that she was a mess.

She needed a haircut and her eyes were swollen and sore from crying. She looked lost in her rumpled clothes. It was -4°C, according to the BBC, and she was shivering in a flimsy denim jacket, navy bootcut jeans that were soaked through, and filthy Adidas trainers. She followed me into the kitchen and sat down at the table.

'You've got your GCSEs soon,' she said. 'How did your mocks go?'

'Rubbish,' I replied. 'They got messed up with all the snow and the closures. The school had to fit them in on the days we were open. Don't matter though.'

'Yeah – because my little brother is clever.'

I nodded as I put the kettle on. 'You need a warmer coat,' I told her, looking at the jacket she'd hung on the back of her chair.

'Yeah,' she replied with a smile.

My phone buzzed in my pocket. It was Charlotte.

'Mum says you're always out,' Jas went on.

'Typical,' I said. 'She won't be happy until I get a nice wife and some male babies . . .'

Jas half smiled this time before looking away.

'I've *got* a life,' I continued.

'They only want the best for you,' she told me, pushing imaginary crumbs around the table.

'Yeah, me too.'

I started making her tea. The mug was her favourite

– a Bart Simpson one with EAT MY SHORTS on it.

'So how come you're here?' I asked her.

Jas shrugged. 'Do I need a reason?'

'Nah,' I replied. 'I'm not having a go or anything.'

She smiled at me. 'Just checking.'

We went and sat in the living room. The telly was on but we weren't watching it.

'How's Taz?' I asked her.

'He's OK, I suppose. I don't see him much nowadays.'

'Is he busy with work?'

Jas looked away, ignoring the question. She got up, walked over to the fireplace and picked up a photograph that sat on the mantel.

'I remember when this was taken,' she said, turning to face me.

I got up and went over to her, taking the silver frame. The photograph was of me, her and Amar, taken in Florida. I would have been about seven at the time. The three of us were standing together in front of the castle at Disney World, wearing sunglasses, hats and Disney T-shirts. Jas and Amar were smiling but I looked miserable.

'Do you remember how much you cried just before Dad took that?' Jas asked me.

I nodded. 'Yeah. Amar was being a dickhead.'

Jas took the photo frame and held it close to her face. Her honey-coloured eyes grew wider and she smiled to herself. 'I remember – we got hotdogs and he ate half of yours too. And then Dad wouldn't get you another one so you had a tantrum.'

'I didn't have a tantrum!' I protested. 'Amar ate my *hotdog*.'

Jas looked at me and grinned. 'Remember when we got off the plane?'

'How could I forget?' I said. 'Dad was *well* embarrassing. Like when that guy at immigration thought he was an Arab. Dad started shouting and the bloke got his gun out!'

'Yeah . . . Mum was going mental because she thought Dad would get killed,' added Jas.

I smiled back at my sister, trying not to laugh.

'I thought he was gonna explode!' she went on. 'He was complaining all the way to the villa.'

'That was funny.'

She put the photo back and walked over to the window.

'Do you miss being here?' I asked her.

'Yes,' she said quietly. Quickly.

My phone vibrated again. I read the message and typed a reply.

'Another friend?' asked Jas.

I shook my head. 'You may as well know – it's my girlfriend . . .'

Jas's eyes widened and I felt bad that she didn't

know about Charlotte. I didn't keep secrets from my sister.

'*Girlfriend?*'

'Yeah,' I replied. 'She's called Charlotte.'

'Do Mum and Dad know?'

I started laughing. 'Yeah – like they'd be cool with that,' I said. 'Mum would have a heart attack.'

My sister muttered something that I didn't catch.

'I need a shower,' she went on.

'What did you just mumble then?' I asked.

'I left some clothes here last time,' she replied, ignoring my question.

I remember thinking that she was acting weird. That maybe something was wrong. Until I got *another* message from Charlotte – a photo of her boobs. After that, I wasn't thinking about Jas any more.

I was in the conservatory, playing Call of Duty, when Jas came down again. She actually *knocked* on the door before sliding it open.

'I was thinking about my old CDs,' she said.

I killed another soldier with a bayonet before stopping the game. 'You don't have to knock, you nutter,' I said.

'I thought you might—' she began, before catching herself. 'Have you still got my CDs?'

I nodded. 'I transferred all the songs I liked to

iTunes,' I explained. 'But I didn't get rid of them.'

'If I bring my laptop round, can you do that for me too?' she asked.

'Yeah,' I said, 'but you could do it. It's *easy*.'

'I'm hoping to go away,' she told me. 'On holiday. Taz got me an iPod but I don't know what to do with it.'

'*Yeah* . . .' I grinned. 'You and technology, eh?'

'You hungry?' she asked.

'Starving,' I replied, hoping she'd buy me a takeaway.

'I haven't got my car,' she said, stating the obvious.

'I kind of guessed that. The way you looked before was a big giveaway – like a frozen rat.'

'You cheeky little shit!' She half smiled at me. 'You want some food or not?'

I stood up and gave her a big hug. 'Only joking, sis,' I said.

She was wearing grey combats, a red T-shirt and a sky-blue hoodie. Her hair was still damp and smelled of apricots.

'Pizza?' she asked.

I nodded like a little kid. 'Pepperoni!'

And that was it. The last memory I have of Jas. Sitting in the conservatory, drinking Coke Zero, eating pepperoni and black olive pizza and watching crap telly. Talking about the past and telling stupid jokes.

I remember Mum walking in, smelling of onions because she'd been helping to cook at the *gurdwara*. She gave us a funny look, asked if we'd been drinking. When we started giggling, she left us to it. Jas made me watch a chick flick before bed.

When I woke just after lunch time the following day, my sister was gone.

Laura watched a group of drunken Asian men stagger into the bar.

Ricky turned to her and shrugged. 'Them Indians spend good money at the bar,' he explained, wiping a breadcrumb from his black Hugo Boss suit.

Laura was still fuming, having turned the men away, only for one of them to call Ricky. 'So why don't you stand on the door?' she snapped.

'That's your job though, innit?' replied Ricky as Johnny Owens, the unofficial head doorman, grinned at her, his ice-blue eyes unblinking.

'Exactly,' said Laura. 'My job . . . So if I turn people away, it's because I'm doing my job. A job I'm allowed to do – *legally*. Unlike Johnny.'

Ricky looked at her, sniffed and wiped his nose. Laura saw that his pupils were tiny black pinpricks. He'd been at the cocaine already.

'Is Taz in the office?' she asked him.

'Sorting out the VAT figures.'

Laura looked at the clipboard in her hands. 'Here,' she said, handing the guest list to Ricky. 'You stand in the freezing cold and decide which bunch of drunken bums you want to let in.'

'But . . .'

Laura ignored him. She turned into the bar, dodging past a group of middle-aged women — workmates out on the piss. When she found that the office was locked, it didn't help her mood. She balled her right hand into a fist and thumped on the heavy door. Eventually it opened and an angry-looking Taz appeared.

'What?' he snapped, turning back to his desk.

'Are you busy?' Laura walked in and closed the door behind her.

A mountain of paperwork sat on the desk. She pulled up a chair and looked at the mess. Unfiled receipts and invoices lay piled high, and next to them were some ledger books, bound in black cardboard with red edging.

'Having fun?' she asked.

'Numbers,' he explained. 'They do my head in . . .'

Laura shrugged. She adjusted the hem of her grey wool dress, worn over black tights, with knee-high black leather boots. 'Get the accountant to do them,' she suggested.

Taz looked at her and smiled. 'Yeah . . .' he said. 'After I've played with them.'

Laura nodded, understanding that Taz was hiding

money. The two account ledgers were secret books in which he noted down funds hidden from the tax office and his accountant. Cash – taken out of the profits and 'reassigned'. Laura knew this because she had helped Taz before. It was a simple system; a system that she understood inside out. A system that allowed her to take money too – behind Taz's back.

'I'm quitting,' she told him. 'I've had enough.'

Taz shook his head, then looked at his expensive silver watch. It matched his steel-grey suit perfectly. Armani and Omega – serious style.

'Like the last time?' he asked, knowing how to wind her up.

'No,' Laura replied through gritted teeth. 'Not like last time . . .'

Taz shrugged. 'You won't leave.'

'I can't stand being here any more. I don't do anything!'

'Course you do something – you run the bar most nights.'

Laura sighed. 'No,' she said. 'You run the bar. I make decisions, and you or your brother ignore them. Like just now . . .'

Taz raised an eyebrow. 'What happened just now?'

'The usual. A bunch of pissed-up Asian blokes come along, I turn them away, and Ricky lets them in.'

'They spend money,' said Taz, parroting his brother.

'Fuck their money!' yelled Laura. 'I don't care about their money or whether they're your uncle's cousin's brother!'

'What you on about?' Taz tried not to grin.

'That Asian thing you lot do. Like every other Asian who comes to the door knows you or is related . . .'

Taz shrugged. 'That's 'cos loads of them are. That's the way things work with us Asians.'

'Yeah, but I don't see why *I* should have to deal with it.'

Taz stood up and walked round the desk to face her. 'Like you have to deal with the cash?'

'Get stuffed, you twat!' she yelled, pitching forwards in her chair.

Taz tried to calm down. It didn't work. 'Let's see . . .' he hissed. 'You get paid twice what you'd get anywhere else. You get taken on expensive holidays and live rent-free in my flat. That car you drive is paid for, even the bastard diesel that goes into it, and you're complaining?'

'You always throw that in my face,' complained Laura. 'I didn't ask you for all that. You chose to do it!'

'And you love it,' replied Taz. 'So don't sit there and get on no high horse . . .'

Laura stood up and confronted him. 'Like I said, I *quit*.'

She grabbed her jacket from behind Ricky's desk, picked up her car keys and stormed out of the office.

'Yeah — get out, you little bitch!' Taz shouted after her. 'It's my car you're getting into and my flat you're going home to. You'll be on the phone tomorrow, crying 'bout being sorry.'

Laura kicked open the fire exit to the car park and let the chill wind cool her down. Then, with tears in her eyes, she got into her Mini Cooper, paid for by Taz, and went home to his flat.

SEVEN

A month after I last saw Jas, things went wrong. She hadn't been round but I knew she'd phoned Mum a few times. Not seeing her didn't worry me. I just assumed that she was busy. I didn't even think about it, not until much later. But by then it was too late.

I wanted to get home from school, dump my stuff and check on Charlotte, who was ill. When I saw my dad's shiny blue Mercedes on our drive, I knew instantly that something was up. Dad worked long hours – he was never home in the afternoon. Never. Amar and Taz had parked on the drive too. Charlotte slipped from my mind, replaced by thoughts of my sister.

Amar opened the door, his face like thunder. His forehead was creased, his eyes glazed from too many shots of Chivas.

'What's goin' on?' I asked him, shrugging off my kitbag.

'Nothing,' he said. 'Just go to your room.'

'Don't tell me what to do,' I replied angrily. '*You* ain't my dad.'

Normally my brother would have stood his ground and argued. That day, he just shook his head and went back into the room my parents kept for guests. He closed the door behind him.

I took off my jacket, went into the kitchen and hung it up. Then I removed my trainers, sliding across the dark wooden floor, back into the hallway. The stairs rose in the middle, opposite the front door. On one side were a living room and a dining room. The front room was opposite, and behind it lay a second living room, the kitchen and the conservatory.

I heard raised voices from the front room and decided to investigate. My dad was sitting on the large chocolate-brown sofa, next to Taz and Ricky. Each held a glass of Chivas. Dad's face was red with anger. He saw me and shook his head. I started getting paranoid, thinking that I'd done something wrong. Only Taz and Ricky's presence didn't make sense. It couldn't be about me.

My mum sat opposite Dad. Next to her were Taz's mum and sister. The woman who'd help arrange Jas's wedding sat with them – short, fat and middle-aged, wearing a green outfit and a look of disgust. Mum sat with her head bowed. She looked like she had been crying.

'What's going on?' I asked.

By that point I knew there must be a problem with Jas. I just didn't know what it was. 'Where's my sister?' I added.

No one spoke at first. Then Ricky stood up and came

over to me. He was wearing a shiny metal-grey suit at least one size too small. The trousers looked like they would burst, stretched over on his huge thighs. He put his meaty hand on my shoulder. For a second I looked at the gold rings he was wearing. Fat things that looked well expensive.

'What can I say, bro?'

I pulled away and looked him in the eye. 'About what? Where's my sister?' I asked again.

'That's why we're here,' said Ricky. 'She's done a runner, innit.'

Without realizing what I was doing, I shook my head. 'What do you mean?' I looked at Amar. Jas had mentioned a holiday last time I'd seen her. A pang of guilt hit me as I remembered her iPod. I had totally forgotten about it.

Amar was standing by the window, leaning on the sill. He straightened up. 'She left home,' he said softly. 'Ran off . . .'

'Why would she run off?' I stared at Taz. The dark circles under his eyes were puffy and swollen. He picked up his glass of whisky and looked at it.

'Well?' I asked. 'She said she was going on holiday.'

'She ain't on holiday,' Amar insisted.

'She waited until we were all out,' Ricky explained. 'She took a large suitcase, most of her clothes, about five grand in cash and the car—'

69

'No way,' I said.

'She didn't leave a note or anything,' Ricky went on, 'but we know she was planning it.'

I went over to an armchair and sat down. Why would my sister have run away? It wasn't like she was some seven-year-old kid. There had to be something wrong.

'Why?' I asked again.

My dad spoke in Punjabi, told me to shut up.

'No,' I replied. 'I don't believe it . . .'

'They found emails and text messages and stuff,' Amar told me. 'It's all true.'

I shook my head. 'I know my sister, Amar. *You* do too . . .'

His face fell. He looked down at his feet.

'OK, then,' I heard Taz say, his voice getting louder. 'You tell me this, Sat – if you *know* your sister – why was she seein' some Paki?'

I flew out of my chair, squaring up to him. 'Don't tell lies, you bastard!' I shouted.

Taz looked me in the eye. He reached into the pocket of his expensive-looking dark-grey suit and pulled out some papers. 'Read these, you dickhead!' he spat, throwing them in my face.

I wanted to punch him in the mouth, but suddenly my dad shot to his feet and grabbed me.

'*Out!*' he spat into my face. '*Go to your room!*'

I tried to get past him, get at Taz. My head was

burning with rage. It couldn't be true. It *couldn't* be – not unless Taz was the cause. I *knew* my sister. No way would she have cheated on him. It dawned on me then. They weren't *worried* about Jas. They'd come over because Jas had *embarrassed* them. Or so they said.

'I have been shamed enough today,' Dad added. He let me go, seeming calmer. 'Please don't take the little dignity I have left. Please . . .'

The look on his face nearly made me cry. I stared into his pale brown eyes and realized that he was fighting back tears. Trying desperately to hide the pain and shock. I gave Taz another look, picked up the papers he'd thrown at me and walked out of the room. Behind me, I heard my dad begin to apologize.

I went straight up to my room, slammed the door shut and reached for my mobile. I found my sister's number and dialled. A pre-recorded voice said that the phone was switched off. I tried a few more times with the same result. I threw my mobile on the floor and looked at the papers. They were printouts of texts, Facebook messages and emails, all under our surname, Kooner. Each message was from my sister to some lad with a Muslim name – Azhar Khan. The first text had his number listed next to it. I picked up my phone and dialled, then waited for someone to answer. The line was dead. I tried again, just to be sure, and got the same response. Nothing.

I booted up my computer and logged on to Facebook, searching for Jas's page. It was there, but with no recent activity. The only photo was the profile picture and she didn't have any messages – not public ones, anyway. She only had one friend listed – Azhar Khan; but no picture. I clicked on the link, went to his page. Again, there was nothing; he too had only one friend – Jas.

Later, after Taz had gone, I sat at the garden table, shivering. I couldn't stop thinking about Jas. She had mentioned a holiday when we last spoke – not running away. The printouts from Taz lay in front of me. I picked one of them up. I couldn't believe that my sister had written them. The words were nasty and sexual, and Jas wouldn't have used them. Not unless she had two personalities and had kept one hidden from me. It just didn't make sense. There was no way she'd have lied. Jas didn't know *how* to lie.

Behind me, the kitchen door opened. Without looking, I sensed Amar behind me. I could smell Hugo Boss aftershave – his favourite, a present from Jas. I often used it without asking. I didn't turn round.

'You OK?' he asked.

I didn't respond. Instead, I laid the printout down on the table.

'This is difficult for all of us,' Amar said. 'But you've

got the proof right there—'

'This don't mean shit,' I snapped. 'I tried calling – her phone's off. And the number for that Khan bloke doesn't work either. And what kind of lad has a Facebook page with only one friend listed? It's a con—'

'No,' he said. 'They were hiding their affair so they only used Facebook to contact each other. That way no one would know anything.'

Amar came over and took the chair next to mine. He picked up a printout and looked at it. 'These messages were from Jas's phone,' he pointed out needlessly. I knew they were from her phone.

'Something's wrong,' I said, pulling up the hood of my grey and white Adidas top.

'You can say that again,' replied Amar. 'Dad is in bits and Mum just keeps crying.'

I turned to face him. 'She wouldn't do this. There's just no way . . .'

Amar shrugged. 'How much do we really know?'

'We're talking about *Jas*,' I reminded him.

'We don't know what went on,' he continued. 'Taz said that she'd been acting weird for a while; like she had stuff to hide. That's why he started checking emails and stuff . . .'

I picked up another sheet of evidence and studied it for a moment. 'Why are we even *listening* to Taz?' I asked. 'I mean, she's our *sister*. Surely we should be talking to *her*.'

'We don't know where she is. She didn't come here. She's not answering your calls. She's run off – with another man; a Muslim.'

'Who cares if he's Muslim, Christian or sodding Alien?' I asked angrily.

'You know what Dad is like,' replied Amar.

I did. My dad had many qualities but he was a traditionalist too. For him, Sikh girls married Sikh men, and that was that. They didn't get divorced or run away over affairs. They definitely didn't go off with Muslims. His feelings had more to do with prejudice than with any sense of tradition. It was something I didn't like about him. That's why I hadn't told him about Charlotte.

'Where is he?' I asked.

'Indoors,' said Amar. 'He's just opened another bottle of Chivas.'

I picked up the printouts and stood up. 'I'm going to talk to him,' I said. 'Tell him what I think.'

Amar put his hand on my arm. 'Leave it, Sat,' he warned. 'He's not in the mood.'

Not for the first time, I ignored my brother's advice and went inside. Dad was sitting in the same spot. A plate of food sat untouched on the coffee table, next to an empty bottle of Chivas Regal. He was holding the second bottle, a quarter of it gone.

'Dad . . .' I said.

My old man looked up and shed a few tears. Lifted the bottle to his lips and took a long swig. Unsure of myself, I stood and watched him. He wiped his mouth and sniffed.

'*Dad . . . ?*'

His reply was a gruff whisper, his eyes fixed. 'I did *everything* for my kids. And for *what*? So that my only daughter could spit in my face? Trample my *izzat* in the dirt?'

'But she—' I began.

My dad held up his free hand, silencing me. 'Don't defend her,' he ordered. 'Not when the evidence is thrown in your face like shit! The shame I feel cannot be measured. Your sister has taken my life from me.'

I tried to speak but no words would come.

'*Get out!*' he yelled. 'Before I lose my temper.'

Despite my anger and frustration, I did as he asked.

EIGHT

I skipped school the next day, fending off calls from Charlotte. I wasn't ready to talk to her – or anyone else. I didn't *want* to talk. I passed the time randomly surfing the Internet and listening to music. Amar and Mandy came over around five p.m. As soon as I heard Amar's voice, I went out to confront him.

'We need to call the police,' I said.

'What *for*?' he asked, clearly shocked, his eyes widening as though he'd spotted mushrooms growing out of my head or something.

'Because something's not right. Jas wouldn't just run off, and she definitely wouldn't—'

Amar told me to shut up, taking hold of my shoulders. 'I know it's hard to believe, Sat, but she's gone, OK?'

I tried to pull myself free, shaking my head. 'No!' I shouted. 'Jas wouldn't do that!'

'*Yes!*' Amar shouted back. 'We've seen the evidence, Sat. That's *her* Facebook page, *her* email address—'

'But—'

'Just listen!' he ordered. 'This is destroying our parents. We *have* to stick by them. Help them . . .'

Despite myself, I felt tears coming. My voice started

to falter. 'But it's *Jas*!' I croaked, sounding like a spoiled ten-year-old.

Amar pulled me in to his chest and hugged me. He wiped my face. 'I need a drink,' he told me. 'Mandy's making dinner.'

I nodded. 'Be down in a minute,' I told him, turning back into my room.

Wiping the remaining tears away, I grabbed my mobile phone. I dialled Jas's number again, praying that she would answer. She didn't. I tried repeatedly, but got nothing. Eventually my phone gave up and died on me.

Amar and Mandy were in the kitchen, sitting at the table, when I joined them. Amar was holding a can of Red Stripe.

'Want one?' he asked me.

'I'll get it,' said Mandy, not waiting for my reply.

The *Mail*, Dad's daily newspaper, lay on the table. I glanced at the back pages, skimming through football gossip. Then I turned to the front. The headline was about child abuse. I pushed it away, took the lager Mandy handed me and cracked it open.

'What do *you* think?' I asked her.

Mandy sat down again, shaking her head. 'I don't know what to think. It's all so shocking.'

I took a swig of lager, savouring the bitter taste. 'Do you think Jas would do this?'

Mandy frowned. 'No,' she said. 'It's completely out of character.'

'But it *has* happened,' Amar told us. 'There's no point in lying to ourselves. That won't help anyone.'

I took another gulp of lager, swallowed and looked at my brother. 'Has Dad said anything else?'

'Nah,' replied Amar. 'He went to bed pissed, woke up pissed, then started all over again. I had to go and sort the shops out for him.'

'Where is he?'

'Front room, same as yesterday.'

I thought about going to see him. It must have shown. Amar and Mandy started shaking their heads.

'Don't even think about it,' said my brother. 'The last thing he wants to hear is Jas's name.'

'We can't just let him get drunk every day,' I said.

'Give him a few days,' he replied. 'You know what he's like.'

I ate with them in the kitchen before helping Mandy wash the dishes. Amar stayed sitting at the table.

'Where's Mum?' I asked him.

'Went round to Uncle Sodhi's.'

'Do you think she'll get in touch?'

'Mum?' he asked, pouring himself a large whisky.

'No – Jas.'

'If she *has* gone off with some bloke, she won't call us,' he said.

I knew he was right. My parents were old-fashioned. For them, what Jas had done – *if* she had done it – was dishonourable. They wouldn't forgive her, no matter what. She would know it too. She wouldn't even think of getting in touch.

'I still don't believe it,' I said. 'Remember when she had to leave college? That was all bollocks too.'

'You can deny it all you like,' Amar told me, 'but she's been gone for a week. Now this has happened – who knows about the lad from college? Could be the same man.'

I nearly choked. 'A *week*? But they only came round yesterday.'

Amar shook his head. 'They waited. Taz was hoping she'd come back.'

I couldn't believe what I was hearing. 'Now I *know* there's something wrong,' I told him.

Amar looked pissed off with me. 'Stop it, Sat. Just stop it. Taz ain't some bad man. You've spent time with him – he's a good lad.'

'I don't care what he says,' I replied. 'The only person I give a toss about is Jas.'

Amar sighed. 'Don't you think I care about our sister?' he asked me. 'Don't you think *I'm* gutted too? We can't ignore the evidence though, mate. When I read them messages, I felt sick. My *own* sister . . . destroying our honour.'

Family honour didn't mean a thing to me. Surely Jas was the only one who mattered. How could they take Taz's side over hers?

'I'm going out,' I said.

'Where?' asked Amar.

I shrugged. 'Just out.'

I headed for a Subway and bought myself a Coke, just for something to do. I sat on a dull green seat, staring out of the window. It was a quiet night and very, very cold. Some lads from school were in there too. I nodded at them but said nothing. One of them, Jacob, told me that Charlotte had been looking for me earlier.

'How'd you know?' I asked.

'She's a mate,' he said, scratching his bum-fluff goatee. 'She asked if I'd seen you around.'

'Thanks,' I replied.

'No worries, Sat. You OK?'

I gave him a look. 'Yeah,' I said. 'Why?'

Jacob ran a hand through his shoulder-length blond hair. 'You look stressed.'

'Nuttin' really,' I lied. I wasn't in the mood to talk. 'Just feeling a bit rough.'

Before he could say anything else, I got up and left. I didn't know where I was going – just knew that I wasn't going home. Not for a while, anyway. Too many thoughts were spinning around in my head. Why had

Taz waited a whole week? Why didn't he tell us straight away? How long had things been going wrong?

It began to snow, and the clouds took on an orange-pink hue. The flakes were light, melting as they hit the ground. As I passed a BP petrol station, I wondered whether Taz had hurt my sister. It was no less likely a story than the one he'd told us. I thought about the messages. They just didn't ring true. The language didn't seem real – the words were ones that Jas would never have used; words that she would have found embarrassing or offensive.

Yet how well did I really know my sister? I mean, I *thought* I knew her, but just like me, she would have had secrets. A private life that she didn't tell me about. Eventually I remembered why she'd married Taz in the first place; the problems she'd had at college. Was the man in the messages the same one she'd known at college?

For the next hour I wandered back in the general direction of the house. I took every detour I could before I finally got there. By the time my head hit the pillow I was shivering. My mind was overwhelmed. It was a throbbing jumble of emotions and possibilities, all too painful to bear.

Amanda Ryan yawned as she handed me a cup of coffee. 'I know all this stuff,' she said. 'We covered it two years ago.'

Her one-bedroomed flat was above a fruit and veg shop overlooking a market about ten minutes' walk north-east of St Pancras. To one side of the market there was a council estate. On the other was a giant Royal Mail depot. It was an area of London I didn't know, even though I'd spent many of my weekends visiting Dash, who was at uni in the capital. We were sitting in the living room, decorated in Indian prints and textiles. The room was a rusty red colour, which made it feel small.

'So, in the original story, your family waited a few weeks before going to the police,' she went on.

'Kind of,' I replied.

Amanda looked at me thoughtfully. 'Kind of . . . ?'

'I forced the police on them. They didn't want to talk.'

'Why not?' Her interest was growing.

'Because of the whole "honour" thing. My family wanted

to bury things out of shame. They believed everything that Taz Atwal told them.'

'But you didn't?'

I took a mouthful of coffee, regretting it instantly. 'Shit!'

'It's hot,' said Amanda, trying to suppress a grin. 'That's generally the way it works with boiling water . . .'

'Aren't you having any?' I asked, embarrassed.

'Don't drink it,' she replied. 'Get back to the story.'

'Yeah . . .' I put the mug down on the blonde-coloured floorboards, then waited a moment, trying to get the facts straight in my head.

'Sat?'

'OK — so Jas went missing and all we did was sit around . . .'

'And then what?' Her electric-blue eyes burned into mine.

'I went to ask Taz what had happened. And he went mental . . .'

Amanda looked surprised. 'Why did he react so badly?' She made a note in the A4 pad on her lap.

'Because he had something to hide,' I replied. 'I told him I was going to call the police and report her missing, and he told me not to.'

'Did he give a reason?'

I nodded. 'The same reasons as my family: shame, *izzat* . . .'

'*Izzat* — that's honour, right?'

'Yeah — the great silencer . . .'

She gave me a funny look. 'Why do you say that, Sat?'

'Because it silenced us for two years. That's why I'm here . . .'

'Because you want to make things better?'

I shrugged. 'I can't leave things as they are. See, a few months after Jas went missing, I met someone.'

Amanda made some more notes but didn't reply. She waited for me to continue.

'I met a witness. She told me all about Taz and what happened —'

'Witness to what?' gasped Amanda, her eyes widening with shock.

I picked up the mug. I was about to start something that couldn't be stopped. An avalanche that might blow my family away. I had to do it. I *had* to. When I closed my eyes, Jas was there, always there. I missed her with all my heart, but I knew now that she was never coming back. I wanted to get her face out of my head. I didn't want to forget her. I just wanted some peace . . .

NINE

My parents grew more reclusive. Dad was back at work but he hardly spoke to anyone. In the evenings he just got drunk. Instead of booze, my mum turned to God. She spent her time praying and crying, hiding from the gossip. The *gurdwara* became a no-go area. There were too many people there; too many questions and pitiful looks. My brother and his wife spent most of their time at ours. Mandy took over from Mum, despite being nearly six months pregnant. She did all the cooking and cleaning. Amar became the man of the house. He took over the businesses and made the decisions. My dad manned the tills but he was like a ghost. An empty shell that had stopped caring. Amar had to hold it all together.

I didn't stop talking about Jas, which pissed Amar off. He said I needed to sort my head out – told me to think about my parents. I *did* try to speak to them, but they weren't interested. Dad would sit on his own, bottle in hand, crying. Mum told me not to bother her. She shouted at me whenever I talked about my sister. My family was falling apart and I didn't like it – but I couldn't stop it. In fact, I just made it worse.

I couldn't think of anything but Jas. At school I just

sat in silence. I couldn't concentrate and nothing sank in. I was heading for failure and I didn't care. Charlotte knew something was up, and one evening I let it all out. We were in her bedroom, hanging out, when she asked about Jas. Her mum was away with work – her dad had left them a few years earlier.

'There's a rumour going round,' she said, looking sheepish. She was sitting on her bed, legs crossed, feet bare, wearing a scarlet jersey dress over jeans, with no bra. I sat next to her, my back to the wall.

'What rumour?' I snapped.

Charlotte's face fell and I put my hand on her thigh.

'I'm sorry,' I told her. 'Shouldn't have spoken to you like that.'

'I was going to tell you,' she said. 'But you've been so distant . . .'

Her eyes looked sad and I moved in, kissed her on the cheek.

'There's stuff going on,' I explained.

Charlotte nodded. 'The rumour is about Jas leaving her husband.'

'Oh,' I replied. The Punjabi community in Leicester was tight-knit and people were obviously talking. The very thing my parents had been dreading.

'Is it true?'

I shrugged. 'I dunno. Taz reckons she was having an affair. That's what he told my parents.'

'*Really?*'

'I don't believe him,' I went on. 'Jas wasn't like that.'

Charlotte shifted position and lay down on her side. I joined her so that our faces were centimetres apart. I could smell the rosemary and garlic on her breath, feel its heat.

'Smelly . . .' I joked without conviction.

'Better than yours,' she replied. 'Besides, my lunch was gorgeous.'

'Bit like you,' I said.

'I told you when we met – no cheese, please . . .'

'Sorry.' I worked my hand up under her dress, found the small of her back.

'So have you heard from Jas?' she asked.

I looked at her. 'No. No one's heard anything.'

'Have you tried—?'

'Yeah – her phone is switched off.'

Charlotte looked suspicious. 'Off?' she said. 'Isn't that a bit odd?'

'Why?'

'She might not care about Taz, but surely she'd talk to *you*?'

I nodded. 'That's what I thought. But my family don't care.'

'Why not?' asked Charlotte. 'She's your *sister*.'

She sensed my tears before they'd even started. She held me close to her and kissed my mouth.

'What's wrong?' she whispered. 'Tell me . . .'

Charlotte advised me to speak to Taz. We were lying naked under the covers, facing each other. For the first time since Jas had disappeared, I felt calm.

'What for?' I asked her, caressing her thigh. Her skin was hot and sticky.

'Ask him about it . . . Maybe something else has happened,' she continued. 'She might be in trouble.'

'That's what I've been worried about. It just doesn't feel right. Jas would never have run off with some Muslim . . .'

Charlotte's eyes asked me a question.

'It's just a Sikh thing,' I told her, hoping she wouldn't push it.

I didn't know how to explain. My family's concept of honour was so different to anything Charlotte would understand. My dad's prejudice against other religions. The backward view of women and what they were supposed to do. It sounded stupid to me; Charlotte would think it was barbaric. No one would ever dictate her morals to her – tell her who she could sleep with or marry. She'd never understand Jas's life or her choices. Despite being born and raised in Leicester, Jas had to be an Indian girl. The British thing – going out, living with boyfriends, sex before marriage – went against my parents' traditions. They would never have accepted it.

It was different for me. I didn't have the same restrictions. Eventually my parents would want me to settle down, just like Amar. I was male though – the *izzat* thing was easier for me. I could never have lived Jas's life. It would have driven me mad. I began to hope that she *had* run away. Perhaps it was the only option she had. The only way she could be free to live her own life.

Only I didn't believe she'd done that. I would end up doing it, for sure. I was never going to bow to my parents' demands. I wanted to move out, get a good job, explore what the world had to offer. But Jas wasn't like me and she never had been. There was something wrong and I had to find out what.

'You're right,' I told Charlotte. 'About confronting Taz.'

'When?' she asked.

'Friday night. You wanna come? We could go out after . . .'

Charlotte shook her head. 'I'd love to, but I can't.'

'Why not?'

'Coursework. You've got the same deadline, remember?'

I shook my head. 'School can wait,' I told her. 'I can't concentrate anyway. I have to find out about Jas . . .'

'You'll fail the exams,' she said.

I shrugged. 'I can always do them again.'

A cloud of disappointment crossed Charlotte's face. She sighed and turned away from me.

'Char . . . ?'

'I don't want you to fail,' she told me. 'I can't watch you fail.'

But I wasn't listening properly. I left Charlotte's around midnight and thought about Jas all the way home.

When she asks him where he's been, he sneers at her.

'None of your business,' he tells her.

She knows that she shouldn't push it. He has already shown her that his fists do the talking. Except she's had enough. Enough of the nights when he comes in stinking of booze and cigarettes and other women. The nights when he doesn't come home at all. The long weekends away and the business trips to Spain or wherever.

Then there are the nights when he comes in with his face contorted and his eyes wide and wild. Sniffing and sneezing constantly, and disappearing into the bathroom every ten minutes. The nights when he takes what he wants and leaves her beaten and bleeding and torn. When he forces her to do things, grunting in satisfaction as he watches her debase herself. A casualty of his addiction to depravity. No matter how much she cries and wails, he takes no pity. No one comes to her aid. No one else notices the bruises, hears the screams or sees the way she limps around. No one dares to question him. Instead, they treat him with kid gloves, as though scared of what he might do.

It's taken her a few months to realize that he is a monster, but now that she knows, she cannot think of anything else. She knows that she must leave. Knows that if she doesn't, he'll kill her. Though leaving will only bring shame, and she doesn't want that. Not for her mother or her father, and certainly not for her brothers. Yet what choice does she have? What alternative has he left her?

What she needs is help. She needs someone to listen to her pleas, to come to her aid and take pity on her miserable existence. What she needs is a plan. Something that will help her to get away. Until then she is stuck in a weird kind of limbo. Stuck with him . . .

'Do you think I'm stupid?' she asks him. 'I *know* what you are. I know what you do – how you make your money.'

He looks over at her, shakes his head. 'How many times?' he says. 'How many fucking times do I have to show you?'

She doesn't move, doesn't flinch. Even though she knows what is coming. Knows that he is about to leave her with more bruises.

The first punch staggers her and sends needles of pain searing through her body. The second, although just as powerful, is easier for her to bear. By the time she hits the floor, bleeding and whimpering, he is on the tenth or eleventh blow and she has stopped feeling anything at all. Instead, she closes her eyes and tries to picture better times. Better times past and better times yet to come.

TEN

'Not tonight.'

The bouncer from New Year's Eve smirked at me. For a moment I thought he'd recognized me. He hadn't. I'd downed a few shots with Dash in Oadby before heading into town alone. My head was light and I was nervous.

'What?' I asked, remembering the crap he'd given me last time.

'I *said* not tonight.'

'I'm here to see Taz Atwal,' I told him. 'Just go and get him . . .'

The doorman had a face like carved stone, with a massive forehead and square jaw. A flat and broken boxer's nose sat underneath dead, soulless eyes. The shape of his head reminded me of those Easter Island statues.

'I don't take orders,' he sneered. 'Not from kids.'

I glared at him, hoping to cover up my nerves. My stomach was flipping around like a dying fish. 'Just get him,' I demanded. 'Or do you want *me* to call him?'

He shrugged. 'Do what you like,' he said, turning to the other bouncer, who was half his size and nowhere near as scary.

I swore at him under my breath and dialled Taz. 'It's Sat,' I said.

'Yeah, I know,' he snapped. 'I can see you on the CCTV.'

'I'm outside. Let me in . . .'

I heard Taz sigh and then whisper to someone. 'Go home, Sat,' he replied eventually. 'I'm busy, mate.'

'No. I wanna talk to you.'

'About what?'

'My sister,' I said, lowering my voice. 'I *know* you did something to her . . .'

Taz waited before replying. 'OK. See the side alley being blocked by a red BMW?'

I turned to my left and saw the car. 'Yeah – what about it?'

'Go to the back door. I'll be out in a minute.'

I put my phone away and looked at the bouncer. 'Oi!' I shouted.

He turned his huge head. 'Something I can help you with?' he said in a low voice.

'Getting in,' I bragged like a dickhead. 'You gonna stop me now?'

He caught himself just before rage kicked in, and calmed down. 'Lucky you,' he said. 'Now off you toddle . . .'

He waved me away and started laughing.

Taz was waiting. He wore a dark grey suit with a

matching shirt and tie. He looked drunk. A barman was wheeling a large blue bin past us. He didn't look up.

'What?' Taz asked, clearly annoyed.

'I know you did something to Jas,' I said without thinking. Everything I'd planned to say on the way over had slipped from my mind.

'Oh yeah?' he asked, screwing up his face.

'Yeah.'

Taz put his hands in his trouser pockets and spat something out of his mouth. He looked me in the eye. 'What did I do?' he demanded. *What?*

'I dunno . . .' I felt as ridiculous as I sounded. 'But I know it was *something*.'

Taz's face relaxed. He came towards me and put a hand on my shoulder. 'I know it's hard,' he said, his voice changing completely. 'But you need to go home, Sat.' He sounded like he actually cared.

'I don't want to go home. I want you to *tell* me . . .'

Taz removed his hand and sighed. 'Tell you *what*, mate?'

'About Jas,' I said. 'Why would she run off? What did you *do* to her?'

Taz swore. 'I gave her everything she wanted!' he spat. '*That's* what I did! Big house, nice car, all the money she could spend. And she repaid me by running off with a Paki!'

I shook my head. 'No, she didn't,' I said. 'I know,

Taz . . . I know . . .'

That was when I saw it – in his face, his eyes. A sign of recognition, maybe even guilt. It was only there for a moment, but that was long enough. Then, just like his bouncer, he caught himself and his expression changed.

'You ain't got a clue what you're talking about, bro,' he replied, almost in a whisper. 'If I was you, I'd keep my mouth shut, you get me?'

I felt my legs begin to wobble. My mouth went dry. 'Why? Why should I keep my mouth shut?'

He looked around the car park before replying. We were alone. ''Cos people with big mouths get sorted,' he told me. 'You cause any trouble for me or my family—'

'I'm going to the police,' I said, surprising myself.

'You what?'

'The police,' I repeated. 'You're hiding something and I want to know—'

Suddenly he grabbed hold of my shirt. 'Stay out of it!' he hissed. His eyes burned with rage. He stank of fags and whisky, and something else. Perfume . . .

I struggled with him but he was too strong. I felt weak and useless, angry with myself.

'Your bitch sister has caused enough shame,' he warned. 'Don't make any more trouble for your parents . . .'

'My parents?'

100

'You'll see.' He pushed me away. I stumbled backwards, the Jaguar breaking my fall.

'Keep talking shit and you'll find out,' Taz went on. 'Now fuck off and don't come back here.'

I felt someone grab me by the collar. The bouncer.

'You want me to deal wiv 'im?' he asked Taz.

As he dragged me away, I heard Taz say no.

'But next time, Johnny,' Taz added, 'you can kick the living shit out of him – I don't care. I just don't wanna see his face around here – ever.'

'I'm gonna get you!' I shouted as Johnny threw me out into the street.

I landed on my knees in the middle of the road, facing the traffic. A gleaming white Audi A3 stopped only a couple of metres from my chest.

'*Gerrout the road, you dick!*' the driver shouted from his open window.

I got to my feet, gave the bouncer a last look and walked off into the night.

Laura put the bucket of sawdust back in the cleaning cupboard, went behind the bar and washed her hands. The sawdust dried up fresh vomit, and she was sick of having to use it – though Taz and Ricky were oblivious to the damage their door policy was doing. Bars and clubs survived on their reputation, as Laura had pointed out repeatedly. Her dad had been a pub landlord and she knew the business. Punters loved to talk. What they said about you was important. Puking teenagers did not look good.

Dice had once been the place to go, one of the best bars in town. Over the course of three years, however, since Taz and Ricky had hooked up with Johnny Owens, cocaine and all the other stuff, Dice's reputation had suffered. Now they relied on rowdy blokes, hen parties and teenagers to make money. Wannabe gangsters lurked in every corner and sold drugs from the toilets. Not that it was doing badly. Alongside Taz's other bar and the nightclub, Dice made money. Only that wasn't enough, and Laura knew it. Eventually the handful of nice punters who still came to Dice would leave too, and it would end up a dive. The kind of place that normal, decent drinkers avoided.

Taz just didn't care. He wasn't bothered by Dice's reputation. A place for pissheads, cokeheads, gangsters and their girlfriends, and fat, sweaty businessmen who thought any woman could be bought with a few drinks, a gram of powder and a fat wallet. If anything, Taz seemed to like the rep he was getting. He enjoyed it. People knew who he was and they knew what he could do. He was the man. Just like everything, though, the life Taz was leading went in cycles. One day you were the top dog; the next you were gone, replaced by younger, hungrier, crazier wannabes.

Laura sighed, cussing herself for coming back. She had left so many times, only for Taz to soothe her anger and woo her with sweet words and the promise of a holiday in the sun. She was beginning to hate herself and the life she'd chosen to lead. She wasn't stupid either; Laura knew that she couldn't go on. She would have to leave. Leave or end up a casualty to booze, drugs and the life.

She checked on the bar staff, issued instructions, and then decided to go and check her emails in the office. When she reached the office door, she realized that Taz and Ricky were talking heatedly.

'Forget about it,' she heard Ricky say. 'He don't know shit.'

'Then why was he here?' Taz asked. 'Why was he stressin' me?'

'OK' – Ricky again – 'we'll keep an eye on him. But what's he gonna do, Taz? He don't know what happened.'

'He's callin' the police. That's enough right there.'

The two brothers were silent for a moment, and Laura thought that she'd been discovered. She moved away from the door, which was slightly ajar, ready to make her excuses. Then Ricky spoke up again.

'We stick to the story,' he told his brother. 'Ain't nuttin' the police can do.'

'OK,' said Taz. 'But if he gets in my face again . . .'

'We'll deal with it. Ain't the first time, is it? When I needed that thing gone, you helped me. Now I'm gonna help you back. We're family, innit. Brothers.'

'What about Johnny?'

'What about him?'

'Forget it,' said Taz. 'I'm just a bit para, that's all.'

Laura heard Ricky break into laughter. 'No one is ever gonna find out,' he said. 'We's untouchable, bro. And if them Kooners get in the way, we'll deal with them – you get me?'

'Yeah . . . seems to me like we'll have to,' replied Taz.

'No problem. We gave them the easy option. If we have to step it up, we will. Relax, bro – I'll send that twat a little message. He won't say shit after that. Trus' me, blood.'

Laura decided to leave the emails until later. She found Anton, the bar supervisor, standing just outside the rear fire exit, smoking.

'Has anyone visited Taz tonight?' she asked him.

Anton shrugged. 'Some kid was out here earlier. I was sorting out the empties and I heard them get into it . . .'

'Do you know what it was about?'

'Di'n't really hear,' Anton replied. 'Summat about someone missing, and the lad said he was goin' to the police. Then Johnny come round and dragged him off.'

Laura nodded. 'Thanks, Anton . . . And I didn't ask you shit, OK?'

Anton looked at his boss and laughed. 'None a my business,' he said. 'Specially if you buy me a beer . . .'

ELEVEN

The police officer behind the desk told me to take a seat.

'I'm not sure how much we can do,' she said.

'But I'm reporting a missing person.' A wave of nausea hit me. I thought about my dad, sitting in the dark, crying into a bottle. Doubts began to surface in my mind. Part of me felt like I was betraying my family, but the thought of Jas helped me to deal with the guilt. I took a deep breath and tried to think straight.

'I'm afraid it doesn't work that way,' the policewoman told me.

Her uniform looked boxy and uncomfortable. The skin on her cheeks was blotchy and red. When she realized that I was staring at her, she got self-conscious and rubbed her neck. I looked away.

'Wait here,' she said. 'I'll see if I can find a detective.'

I sat in reception for ten minutes, fighting with my feelings, before a tall female officer came out. She had pale blonde hair cut in a bob, and wore a grey jacket and trousers with a white shirt. There were lines around her light brown eyes and across her forehead. She looked tired.

'I'm Detective Inspector Elliot,' she said. 'Lucy Elliot.'

I stood up and said hello.

'I've got ten minutes,' she told me. 'We can talk in there.'

She pointed towards a light oak door with a small glass panel set into it. Above the window, a plaque read: INTERVIEW ONE. I followed her in. A cheap-looking wooden table stood in the middle of the room, with three ivory-coloured plastic chairs. Posters covered the walls, with information about Crimestoppers and various other things. One of them caught my eye. A bruised female face. The caption underneath said: DON'T SUFFER IN SILENCE.

'Take a seat, Mr Kooner.'

I sat down and thought about what to say. I'd been hoping for longer than ten minutes. 'My sister is missing.'

DI Elliot pulled a spiral notebook and a pen out of her jacket pocket and took the seat opposite mine. 'Before we go on,' she said, 'I have to tell you that unless your sister is a child, we can't really do very much. From what the officer on reception told me, that seems to be the case here.'

I nodded. 'I understand that,' I told her. 'But I want you to know anyway.'

DI Elliot gave me a funny look and then asked me to explain what had happened. I told her everything I knew, while she made notes. Very quickly I realized how stupid I sounded. I was talking about a grown woman and had no evidence of anything criminal. When I finished explaining, Elliot closed her notebook and put it down on the table.

'So,' she asked, 'why do you think something is wrong?'

'My sister wouldn't just leave like that,' I replied. 'I know her.'

Lucy Elliot nodded. 'I understand, but she *is* an adult. Perhaps the simplest explanation is the truth – the one that your brother-in-law gave. Maybe she *has* run off with her lover—'

'No.' I shook my head. 'My sister is traditional. She never had boyfriends and she wouldn't have done anything to disrespect my parents.'

Elliot's eyes widened slightly. Despite the wrinkles and weariness, she was very pretty. 'When you say *traditional*,' she began, 'what do you mean?'

I thought for a moment. What was I trying to say? 'My parents are Sikhs,' I explained. 'They're, like, old school. In my family they frown on having relationships outside marriage.'

'OK,' said DI Elliot, opening her notebook again.

'My older brother married someone from the same background. Jas did the same. They're both very respectful of my parents' wishes. I'm the only one who isn't.'

'And because of these traditions, you're saying that

your sister wouldn't have run off?'

I nodded. 'Exactly . . . especially not with some Muslim.'

Elliot raised an eyebrow.

'It's not racist or anything,' I said quickly. 'It's just that Sikhs don't go out with Muslims and vice versa – not in my family, anyway. There's this stupid prejudice between the two communities 'cos of India and Pakistan and all that stuff.'

'OK,' replied DI Elliot, making more notes. 'Is there anything else you can tell me?'

I stopped and considered what I'd told her so far. There wasn't anything else to add. 'My brother-in-law's reaction was weird,' I pointed out. 'Why would he grab me like he did?'

'Maybe he was angry. His wife has run off with her lover and he's upset. And you go round and accuse *him* of something . . .'

'But he warned me off. He used threats.'

'Were there any witnesses?'

I shook my head. 'No one who heard us.' The only other people in the yard had been the barman and the bouncer called Johnny. The barman ignored us and the bouncer would never say anything. Neither were worth mentioning.

'OK,' she said. 'Nothing we can do there, either. It's your word against his.'

'Yeah . . .'

DI Elliot looked pensive for a while and then asked me how long Jas had been gone.

'Over eight weeks.'

'And she hasn't been in touch with anyone?'

I shook my head.

'No friends or cousins or anyone like that?'

I shook my head again. 'We were really close,' I said. 'She would never hide anything from me.'

'OK, Mr Kooner, here's what I'm going to do. I've made notes of everything you've said and I'm going to pass them on to our Domestic Unit—'

'Domestic?'

'Yes. We have officers who are trained to deal with these kinds of issues; issues where the family are involved.'

I didn't understand. 'How do you mean *involved*?'

'The unit handles domestic abuse cases – cases where there are cultural issues at stake and various things like that . . .'

'Oh, OK,' I replied.

'What I need from you are the full names and addresses of the people involved.'

I gave her the names of all the people in my immediate family, and our address. Next, I gave her both Jas's surnames, Kooner and Atwal. Finally I added my brother-in-law's details.

'Taswinder Atwal,' she repeated.

'Yeah . . . why?'

'Oh, nothing . . .' She smiled at me. 'Just heard the name.'

'He runs some bars in town,' I told her. 'A nightclub too. Maybe you've been . . .'

DI Elliot put away the notebook and pen. 'I don't have time for going out,' she joked. 'Too many *crimes* to solve. Someone from Domestic might want to follow up,' she added more seriously.

I nodded and thanked her.

'But don't get too worked up, Mr Kooner. People go off all the time, and most of them turn up again. As I said, your sister is an adult, so I'm afraid there's very little we can do.'

I thanked her again as she walked me outside. I watched her go back and speak to the desk officer, who shook her head in reply. DI Elliot took out her mobile phone and made a call. I turned round and left her to it.

TWELVE

The Domestic Unit turned up the following Saturday. As soon as I heard the doorbell, I sat up in bed, feeling confused. I'd been dreaming about my sister, asking her to take me to Disney World. I was fully grown in my dream, but I spoke like a child. It was a weird sensation. I shook the remnants of the dream from my head and got out of bed.

From the bathroom I could hear Amar telling someone that he didn't understand. Someone mentioned my name and the report about Jas. I splashed some water on my face, dressed quickly and made my way downstairs.

Two police officers were sitting at the kitchen table, turning down Mandy's offer of tea. Amar looked up and gave me a dirty look. I shrugged at him.

'I'm Satinder Kooner,' I told the police officers, one male, one female.

The woman, who introduced herself as WPC Wright, had cropped chestnut hair and a round face. She smiled and said they were following up my report. 'It's just routine, Mr Kooner,' she added, looking from me to Amar and back again.

The male copper, PC Flack, opened a notebook similar to DI Elliot's and went through my statement. He was a big man with shoulders that were trying to break out of his jacket. His hair was blond and shaved close to the scalp, and he had odd ears that stuck out, with ridges of folded skin like melted plastic. I guessed that he was a rugby player. He was pink around the cheeks, chin and neck, his skin spotted with shaving cuts.

'Mr Satinder Kooner made a report about his sister, a Mrs Jaswinder Atwal, claiming that she went missing on . . .' He studied his notes carefully and read out the date Taz had come to see us.

'No, that's not right,' I told him. 'Taz Atwal *told* us on that day. He waited a week before letting us know about Jas. At least, that's what he said . . .'

The copper looked at Amar. 'Is that correct, Mr Kooner?' he asked.

'Call me Amar,' my brother replied. 'And yes, that sounds right.'

'And she hasn't made any contact with your family since then?'

Amar shook his head, looking over at Mandy.

'And as far as you're aware, Mrs Jaswinder Atwal left her home to be with a Mr' – again PC Flack looked at his notes to be sure – 'a Mr Azhar Khan?'

Amar looked at me before nodding. 'Yes, that's right,' he said. I sensed my brother's anger and I knew I was in trouble.

'And is there anything else that you'd like to add?'

PC Flack asked Amar.

My brother shook his head. The policeman closed his notebook before looking to his partner. WPC Wright nodded, even though he hadn't spoken, and turned to face me.

'The problem we have, Mr Kooner, is this: there is nothing to suggest that your sister has come to any harm. There's no evidence of foul play. Outwardly it seems that your sister has gone off with her lover.'

I frowned. 'You don't get it,' I told her. 'Jas would never do that!'

WPC Wright smiled warmly but it didn't help.

'There is evidence,' said Amar.

'Evidence of what, Mr Kooner?' asked PC Flack.

'Taz gave us copies of emails and text messages that she sent to this . . . man.'

'To Mr Khan?' added WPC Wright.

'Yes,' replied Amar, his face set in disgust. 'So we *know* what she did. If I'm honest, we don't *want* to see her again . . .'

She looked surprised. 'You don't *want* to see your sister?' she asked, incredulous.

Amar sighed. 'You don't understand our community,' he told her. 'What she's done . . . it's not right. She's disgraced us, and she knows it. That's why she ran off, and that's why she won't ever come back. It's her choice.'

I groaned and told my brother to shut up. 'He's just

angry,' I told the police officers. 'He doesn't mean it.'
I turned to my sister-in-law for support but she avoided my eyes.

'*Yes I do!*' Amar yelled, and Mandy placed a hand on his arm.

'OK, you both need to remain calm,' PC Flack ordered.

Amar shook his head. 'Please – Sat is just upset and angry. But he knows the truth. This is a waste of time.'

'Amar—' I began.

'Shut up!' My brother turned to the officers. 'Our sister has run off with some man. She has disgraced our family, and the Atwals too. This is something that can't be fixed. Our parents are distraught – do you understand? This can't be resolved on a talk show or with counselling. She has cut her ties with us and that's the end of it . . .' He stopped to make sure that the officers were listening to him.

'No one *asked* her to go. No one *made* her leave. She *chose* to do it. And, despite what my kid brother tells you, the family don't want to make a report. She's not missing, officers; she's run off. And that's it.'

WPC Wright nodded and looked at me. 'You've made a report,' she told me, 'so we are obliged to do a follow-up, but I do think that the facts are simple. Whether I understand your community or not,' she added, turning to Amar, 'I appreciate that this is a very difficult time for you all.'

'But—' I started to say, only for PC Flack to cut me off.

'We'll talk to the Atwals. If they corroborate the facts as you've laid them out, then we'll close the file. It will remain on record, and you may, if new information comes to light, get in touch with us. But as things stand, there is nothing illegal occurring here.'

Both officers stood up and shook hands with Amar. Then they turned to me.

'I appreciate your concern,' said WPC Wright. 'But please try to understand, Satinder. Adults do surprising things all the time. I'm afraid it's just the way life is.'

I told her she was wrong. 'You're *all* wrong,' I added. 'Something *has* happened to my sister and patronizing me ain't gonna help!'

'*Enough, Sat!*' yelled Amar. He apologized to the officers and led them out.

I looked at Mandy and sighed. Then I turned and put the kettle on; I didn't hear Amar come back in. Suddenly he grabbed my arms and pushed me up against the fridge.

'*You stupid little prick!*' he yelled.

'Get off!' I shouted back, trying to break free, but Amar held me in place.

'You think Dad ain't got enough worries? Forty grand, the wedding cost him – all gone to shit. And what about the Atwals? First our sister disgraces them, and then we send the coppers round? Are you fucking stupid, Sat?'

I tried again to push him away. He was too angry and too strong.

'She ran off with a Paki!' he spat. 'A dirty, stinking *Paki* – I hope she's *dead*!'

'You don't mean that!' I was almost begging him.

'Try me, you little bastard. One more word and I'll batter you!'

At last Mandy decided to intervene. 'Leave him alone, Amar,' she said, grabbing hold of my brother's arms. 'He's a kid – he don't understand.'

Amar relaxed his grip as he replied, his voice breaking. 'He *should* understand. He's not a baby, Mandy. He can see what she's done! He can see Mum crying all day and Dad drinking himself stupid.'

Anger turned to tears and I started to cry. I rushed out of the kitchen, grabbed my jacket and left the house.

I spent the afternoon just walking around Oadby, feeling like shit. I thought about calling Charlotte but decided against it. I was in a foul mood and I didn't want to ruin her day too. Part of me felt ashamed. Amar's words had hurt. I knew that my parents were troubled, but I hadn't meant to cause anyone pain. I'd only gone to the police for Jas; to try to find out what had happened to her. She *was* my sister, after all.

I was angry too – livid. I couldn't understand why Amar had sided with Taz. How could he believe *him* more easily than our sister? And how could Jas change so quickly? Like, one minute she's home-loving and respectful, and the next she's running around having an affair? It just didn't make sense. I wanted to bang Amar's head against a wall, shake him until he woke up. He was betraying Jas – they all were. I was the only one thinking about her. And that wasn't right.

I got home just as the Premier League results came in. Usually I'd have been glued to the telly, but now I couldn't have cared less. I went up to my room and aimlessly surfed around the Internet, clicking on stuff without really paying attention. Half an hour later my dad walked in without knocking. I swivelled in my chair to face him.

'I didn't mean to hurt anyone,' I said, hoping that he'd see how upset I was.

He didn't. He came towards me, eyes ablaze, and slapped me. Pain exploded across my face; my eyes watered and my heart began to pound furiously.

'*You stupid bastard!*'

I started to speak, to defend myself, but it was no good. Dad shook his head in disgust and left the room.

'That's all there is to it,' said Taz, hoping that the coppers had heard enough.

'So you didn't know your wife was having an affair?' asked the female one with the lesbian haircut.

Taz gave her a dirty look. 'If I'd known about it,' he replied, 'I would have said summat, wouldn't I?'

She nodded.

'And you don't know where she went?' asked the man. He was kind of big and Taz wondered whether he was there to intimidate. If he was, it wasn't working.

'I don't know and I don't care. She can bollocks . . .'

The woman told Taz that they were finished.

'Good,' he replied. 'I've got businesses to run.'

They were sitting by the windows, at the front of the bar. Laura was helping the staff prepare for the evening crowd. It was mid-afternoon and there were few customers. Taz wondered where his brother was. They needed to have a serious chat.

'Anything else comes up,' said the male copper, 'or if you remember anything, give us a call.' He dropped a card onto the table.

Taz wondered if he'd done the same at the Kooners' house. 'Yeah, yeah,' he replied.

Once they were gone, he picked up the card and looked at it. Then, even though he wanted to burn it, he pocketed it. It was better to know who he was dealing with than ignore them. If something came up, that is. He saw Laura walking over, and sighed.

'What did they want?' she asked.

Taz shrugged, wishing she would go away. He was tired and tetchy and he needed a shot. 'Just the usual,' he lied. 'They work in bar liaison. They were telling me about a new scheme to control football hooligans when City play at home.'

Laura frowned. 'They look new,' she replied. 'The last two were different.'

Laura knew who the bar liaison officers were. She also knew that they hadn't changed jobs. Taz was lying to her. She thought about what Anton had said – the trouble out in the yard; the conversation she'd overheard between the brothers. Her mind flashed back to New Year's Eve and Taz's brother-in-law. The kid's name was there, on that clipboard she'd held, part of the guest list. Something starting with a K. Ricky had also mentioned a name when she'd been listening by the office door. Kooner . . .

'Oh, shit . . .' she whispered as another image appeared in her head. Sitting on her sofa, drunk and stoned, typing out Facebook messages dictated by Taz, giggling.

'What's that?' asked Taz.

'Nothing . . . I forgot to order mixers . . . I'll do it now.'

She left him to his business.

Twenty minutes later Taz and Ricky were walking across Victoria Park. It lay just south of Leicester's centre, next to the university and De Montfort Hall. Taz shivered as he spoke, his navy suit doing nothing to keep out the winter chill.

'What do you think?' he asked Ricky.

Ricky shrugged. 'Sounded routine to me. That little prick has called them and they've followed up, that's all. Sat don't know shit, so what can he tell them?'

'I warned him, though,' said Taz. 'He should have listened. Now, if I don't do summat I'm gonna look like a pussy.'

Ricky nodded. 'We'll sort it,' he replied.

They watched a huge Alsatian dragging a middle-aged woman across the grass.

'That dog needs a bigger bitch,' Ricky said with a

smirk.

'No time for jokes.' Taz rubbed his hands together. 'Them Kooners are taking the piss. Something has to be done.'

Ricky told him to calm down. 'In time, bro . . . Come – leave the bars to the staff tonight. Laura can handle things, and Johnny's at the club. Let's go to Birmingham and get a couple of slappers – on me.'

Taz smiled. 'Sounds like a plan.'

Ricky took out his mobile, dialled Johnny Owens and told him that he was running things today.

'Call Laura too,' said Taz after Ricky had finished.

'You call her. She's your bit.'

Taz shook his head. 'Not for much longer – not the way she's going . . .'

THIRTEEN

Over the following week, only Mandy spoke to me. Amar and my parents didn't say a thing. Each time I walked into a room, they stopped talking or left. After two days I gave up trying. I spent my time with Dash and Charlotte, or alone in my bedroom, surfing the Net. I even went back to school, although that caused problems too. I'd missed a lot of days and my year head, Mr Wilkinson, was all over me. On the Wednesday of that week, he called me into his office.

'Lots of unexplained absences, Sat,' he said as I took a seat. 'Not to mention your terrible mock results.'

I nodded. 'There's been stuff going on at home,' I replied.

Mr Wilkinson ran a hand through thinning brown hair before adjusting his glasses, which had thick, rectangular black frames. 'Can you be more specific?' he asked. 'This is your GCSE year, Sat, and you need to be here.'

'It's kind of private,' I told him.

'There are people you can speak to at school.' He looked concerned.

As much as I wanted my problems to remain private, I also wanted him off my back. 'It's a family thing,' I said, hoping he'd leave it alone.

'What sort of family thing?'

'Personal.'

Mr Wilkinson gave me a funny look before continuing. 'OK,' he said. 'It's obvious that you don't want to talk. However, your GCSEs are just round the corner. You need to consider the future here, Sat.'

'I know, sir. I've just been having a bad time. I'm OK now, though.'

Wilkinson said he'd keep an eye on my attendance and left it at that. I went to maths but I shouldn't have bothered. I couldn't concentrate, though luckily the teacher didn't ask me anything. I just wanted to go home.

Charlotte looked less than pleased when I got to her house. She was wearing black jeans underneath a flowery yellow dress and she looked tired.

'I'm busy,' she said at the door.

'That's not very nice, is it?' I said, half joking.

She sighed and told me to come in. I followed her into the kitchen and took a seat at the table.

'You want a drink?' she asked.

I shook my head. 'Have I done something wrong, babe?'

She took a bottle of water out of the fridge, poured herself a glass and shrugged. 'No,' she replied. 'I'm just trying to concentrate on my exams. Which is what you should be doing, Sat.'

'Wilkinson said the same thing. I'm worried he's gonna call my parents or summat. Although I doubt they'll care at the moment.'

'He's right. Why haven't you been at school?'

I explained about my confrontation with Taz, pointing out that it was her idea. I told her what the police had said; the trouble I'd caused with my family. But she didn't really listen. The more I tried to excuse my absence, the less happy she looked.

'I know it's hard,' she said. 'I *do*.'

I frowned. 'No, you don't. I can't concentrate on anything. It's like nothing matters any more – only Jas. I should have seen what was happening. But I was too obsessed with myself, with what *I* was doing.'

'Does that include me too?' she asked, stroking the glass.

'Maybe . . . I dunno.'

She looked away, towards the window. Her face was set.

'I didn't mean—' I began.

Charlotte sighed again. 'I can't fail my exams,' she said softly. 'I've worked too hard for this. I want to get out of Leicester and do things . . .'

'And my shit is a problem.'

'Right now,' she admitted, 'it is. When the exams are over . . .'

I stood up. 'OK,' I said, shaking my head.

'I don't want to split up,' she insisted. 'We just need to take a break—'

'I said OK. I understood the first time. I'm not thick.'

'That's just it, Sat,' she replied sadly. 'You're not stupid but you are messing things up.'

'She's my *sister*,' I said. 'What am I *supposed* to do?'

As I left Charlotte's, I rang Dash. We met at a busy local pub. Chelsea versus Arsenal was on and we watched most of it. I told Dash what Charlotte had said.

'She's serious about them exams,' he replied.

'Yeah, but still—' I began. Dash shook his head.

'She's been the same with Pooja.'

'I ain't Pooja,' I replied. 'What with my sister and all that . . .'

Dash knew about Jas, but only the basics. I hadn't told him how upset I was or about the suspicions I had about the Atwals. We didn't talk like that – not about anything important. We never had. Only Charlotte knew everything.

Dash looked uncomfortable at the mention of my sister. 'Dunno what to say,' he said.

'It don't matter. I'll deal with it.'

He shook his head. 'I ain't being funny. If you wanna talk, Sat . . .'

This time I shook my head. 'Nothing to say, really,' I lied, hoping to ease his embarrassment.

128

'*Nah!*' he shouted as someone missed a sitter.

I took a swig of my lager and shut up.

About ten minutes after the game I went to the gents, passing some lads I knew. The pub had two zones – bar at the front, restaurant to the rear. The toilets were down a corridor opposite the seated area. I stepped into a cramped, musty space, trying to avoid the puddles on the floor. As I stood at the urinal, the door creaked open behind me. I went on reading an advert on the wall, paying no attention. Then I heard footsteps, smelled strong aftershave.

'Keep the mouth shut, Kooner,' someone said.

Before I could turn round, I felt something crack against my skull. I fell forward and the lights went out.

When I came to, I was lying on white tiles, my jeans and trainers soaked in piss. Dash and a barmaid were standing over me.

'You OK?' asked Dash.

'Yeah,' I croaked, but my head was throbbing.

'Shall I call the coppers?' asked the girl, young and blonde with a silver ring in her left nostril.

I sat up and shook my head, instantly wishing I hadn't. My brain rattled around like a marble in a tin can. 'No,' I told her. 'I dunno who it was, anyway.'

The barmaid asked if I was sure.

I nodded. 'Thanks, though, yeah?'

'No problem,' she said. 'Good job the manager is out. He'd have been on the phone soon as . . .'

Dash helped me to my feet. I thanked him, looking down at my jeans. 'Bollocks.'

The barmaid grinned at me. 'I'll get you a cloth,' she said.

As she left the toilets, Dash asked me what happened.

'Someone just lamped me in the head,' I told him.

'No reason or nothing?'

'Nothing, mate. Just some random arsehole,' I lied.

Even though I hadn't seen my attacker, I'd heard the words from his mouth. There was only one reason why I'd been smacked. It was a warning from Taz and Ricky. It *had* to be.

'I need a shot,' I told Dash.

He frowned. 'Call the police, Sat.'

'Forget it,' I replied. 'I'm OK.'

FOURTEEN

I spent the following day in my room, only leaving for the bathroom or food. I didn't speak to anyone other than Dash, who'd called to check on me. My head still hurt and I felt embarrassed, scared and angry at the same time. I wondered what the regulars at the pub thought of me. Some idiot teenager, staggering back from the toilets, covered in urine. Stupid though it was, I wanted to fight Taz. The macho bit of me was hurting bad. I was so ashamed.

Only I knew that I couldn't get Taz. He had proper backup – people like the thug who'd attacked me. I'd been given a let-off – a warning to shut up. Had he wanted to, my attacker could have killed me, I'm sure. Taz was playing with me, showing me his power. Making clear how weak I was by comparison. I thought about my family, wondered if Taz would go for them too. Could I put them in that situation? Was that what I wanted for them?

Eventually my anger got the better of me. I realized that I had no choice. Sitting around meekly wouldn't bring Jas back. Cowering because the Atwals were so powerful wouldn't tell me where she'd gone, what had happened to her. Taz's warning was *supposed* to make me stop. He expected me to lie down and take it – accept his decision. Only that wasn't going to happen. My sister was missing and I was going to find out why. No thug in a pub toilet was going to stop me.

That was when I realized the truth: Taz was scared of something. My report to the police had made him act. If he had nothing to hide, why send someone after me? Why not just shrug it off and move on? The police had rattled him, I could tell, which meant that I was on to something – I *had* to be. Taz was hiding something and I was going to find out what.

By the evening I felt wired but even more determined to succeed. I sat at my computer, realizing that I could use it in my quest. I searched various missing person sites, hoping to find some clue, but they didn't help. Jas didn't fit any of their criteria for vulnerable people. She wasn't underage or senile and she wasn't a drug addict or suicidal. Not that I knew of.

Eventually I started looking up news about missing women. I typed different word combinations into Google, amazed at what turned up. Stories about young British Asian women who'd gone missing or, in some cases, been killed or injured by their families. Articles about honour killings and domestic abuse which talked of the high suicide rate amongst British Asian women. The stories scared me – made me more determined to find my sister. By midnight I had a splitting headache and very dry mouth. I went down to the kitchen to get some juice. At the foot of the stairs I heard someone in the living room. The door was ajar. I went over and saw my dad sitting there, crying into a bottle of Glenfiddich. I considered trying to talk to him, but decided against it. I would only make it worse. I got my juice and returned to my bedroom.

My phone lay by the keyboard, buzzing. Charlotte had sent me a text. I read it twice before setting my phone down again. A minute later, it buzzed again. Expecting more of the same stuff about being sorry, I opened the message.

TRY SETTING UP F/BOOK PAGE BOUT JAS? MIGHT HELP. XXX

I smiled to myself, thanked Charlotte in my reply, and opened my home page. Setting up a 'Find Jas Kooner' page was quick and easy. I sent it to every contact I had, asking them to pass it on. If Jas *was* using Facebook, she might see the page I'd made. However, I didn't believe what Taz had said. Jas knew nothing about computers or the Internet, so her Facebook page was really odd. She couldn't even work out iTunes. My page was a long shot, but it was all I had.

I set up similar pages on every social network site I could think of – all of them linked back to Facebook. Once I was finished, I went back to the missing person sites. Some were scams, advertised as free but asking for a fee when you tried to register. Ignoring those, I placed Jas's details on the genuine sites, along with a photo. I also sent an email to everyone I knew, outlining the basic facts and giving my mobile number for people with information. Then I sent it to various women's refuges and charities, hoping that she might have made contact with one. When I was finished, my sister's face was all over cyberspace, and I was in danger of upsetting my family once more. Only I was past caring what Amar and the others thought. My only goal was to find my sister.

My Facebook contacts had already started firing back replies, but not about Jas. They wanted to sympathize and say how shocked they were. I looked at a few before returning to sites I had visited before. I re-read some of the articles about missing women for a while, intermittently checking back with Facebook. Suddenly something caught my attention:

BROTHER OF MISSING WOMAN CONTACTS LOCAL MP

Only it wasn't the headline that made me gasp, it was the next line.

Local woman Anita Athwal has been missing for over a year . . .

My heart pounding in my chest, I started reading the piece, which was from the *Derby Evening Telegraph*. Anita Athwal had been married for a year before she had disappeared during a family trip to India. The official story was that she'd run away with her lover, in a carefully planned scheme. Her brother, Dhaminder Singh, had refused to believe it, however. He'd mounted a one-man campaign to find out the truth.

I checked the tagline and wrote down the name of the journalist. I also noted that the story was two years old. Taking into account the year she'd been gone, Anita Athwal had been missing for three years. Two things about the story rang an alarm in my brain. Firstly there was the 'ran off with her lover' cover story. According to her brother, Anita Athwal had been a loyal and home-loving woman. She was a devout Sikh, so it was really unlikely she'd have had any affair.

Second was her married name, Athwal. Jas and Anita's surnames differed by one letter. To me that seemed too much of a coincidence. My suspicions grew. I Googled '*Derby Evening Telegraph*' and got a phone number. Even though it was now late at night, I rang it immediately and got an automated switchboard. Realizing that I had no choice but to wait until morning, I tried to get some sleep.

* * *

After a restless night, I was back on the phone at eight a.m. This time a tired receptionist answered.

'Hi. I'd to speak to, er . . . Jennifer Barton?'

She put me through to another desk. A croaky-voiced man picked up and I repeated my request.

'Be difficult, son,' replied the old man, whose name, apparently, was Jim. 'Jen Barton left us over a year ago.'

'Oh,' I replied. 'It's just that I'm in Leicester and I read an old story by Jennifer and I wanted to—'

'Whoa!' said Jim, interrupting my verbal diarrhoea. 'Did you say Leicester, son?'

'Yeah.'

He started laughing, a soft, wheezy chortle followed by a rough cough.

'What's so funny?' I asked.

'You obviously don't read the *Mercury*, then. Jennifer Barton works there now.'

I thanked Jim for his time as my belly started flip-flopping. I found the *Leicester Mercury*'s number and dialled it. I went through the same process as with the *Telegraph*, only when I got through, Jennifer Barton answered the phone herself. I explained who I was and how I'd found her.

'My sister has gone missing,' I told her, 'and I read an article that you wrote in the *Telegraph* about Anita Athwal and her brother.'

'I remember that well,' she said. 'But I can't see how I can help you. Have you spoken to the police?'

'Yes – they weren't that interested, but it's not that . . .'

'Oh?'

'It's the names,' I said, tense with excitement. 'My sister's married name is Atwal. A-T-W-A-L.'

Jennifer Barton went quiet. I could hear her breathing down the line.

'Atwal and Athwal,' she said. 'That's very interesting.'

'I haven't finished,' I blurted out. 'My sister's husband gave the same reason for her disappearance. Said she ran off with her lover. Only I know that Jas would never *do* that. *Never* – for the same reasons as Anita's brother gave.'

'He was called Rajinder Athwal – Anita's other half,' said Jennifer. 'What's the name of your sister's husband?'

'Taswinder Atwal.'

'Oh,' she said, sounding disappointed. 'For a moment I thought I had old Ricky Athwal by his balls—'

My head nearly exploded. 'Did you say *Ricky*?'

'Yes,' replied Jennifer. 'Rajinder "Ricky" Athwal. Why?'

FIFTEEN

I had never been to the *Leicester Mercury* offices before. They were on the edge of the city centre, in a box-like building. Glass and silver panels had replaced the old grey and yellow fascia – part of ongoing improvements to the city centre. I caught the bus, getting off at the train station. A couple of minutes later, I stood in the reception, asking for Jennifer Barton. I waited five minutes before someone turned up. She looked young but her voice was deep and throaty, as if she had a permanent cold.

She wore a formal dress, in dolphin grey; her skin was pale, like Charlotte's, and her dark hair was cut to frame her face. Her lips were full and pink, even without any make-up, and her eyes were bright blue, unlike any I had ever seen. They were electric, sparkling with life, the azure blue of a warm tropical sea. They looked unreal, impossible.

'I'm Amanda,' she told me. 'I'm training with Jennifer. Come this way.'

I followed her up some stairs and into a huge office. At least thirty desks were crammed in there, each with its own PC. I felt self-conscious as we passed the formally dressed staff, heading for a private office. I was wearing baggy, dark blue jeans, dirty old trainers that had once been white, a black zip-up hoodie by Bench, and a grey beanie.

Jennifer Barton was waiting for us. She said hello and thanked me for coming. She wanted to record our conversation, pointing to a small digital recorder that lay on the table between us. I made no objection.

'It's my memory,' she told me. 'Not what it used to be.'

I nodded, unsure how to respond.

'Amanda is a trainee and she'll be assisting me,' Jennifer added. 'This is her first proper story.'

I turned to Amanda and smiled. She returned my smile and asked me if I wanted a drink.

'Some water, if that's OK,' I replied, mesmerized by her eyes.

Jennifer told me to make myself comfortable. I took off my hat, unzipped my top and sat down.

'So,' she said, 'this is going to be a bit speculative.'

'Er . . .' I began, not really understanding her.

'What I mean, Mr Kooner, is that we don't have any evidence. No proof of wrongdoing or criminal activity.'

'You can call me Sat,' I told her. 'And yeah, I knew that. About the evidence, that is . . .'

Jennifer Barton must have been in her fifties. Her once-blonde hair was going grey, and she had deep lines around her thin-lipped mouth, hazel eyes and forehead.

She wore a black dress over a slim, almost skinny figure. I thought about my mum: she'd gained a lot of weight recently. Jennifer was probably older, I thought, but she looked much younger than Mum. She wore thick rings on the fingers of both hands. I wondered how she could type. Didn't the rings get in the way?

'We need to be careful,' she continued. 'There can't be any accusations of foul play or anything . . . But we *can* ask questions and pose theories.'

I asked her what she meant as Amanda came back with some water in a small white plastic cup.

'For example – we could quote *you*, Sat. You could point out the similarities between Anita Athwal's case and that of your sister. How you were intrigued by the surnames and so on . . .'

'OK,' I replied, suddenly recalling the attack in the pub. I tried to forget about my fear. 'But what about Ricky?'

Jennifer smiled. 'I was coming to that. Amanda?'

The trainee picked up a notebook and read aloud: '*Rajinder Atwal – that's A-T-W-A-L, aka "Ricky" – is joint owner of several businesses, according to Companies House. He lives in Glenfield, just outside Leicester, and has no wife or children. His brother, Taswinder Atwal, same spelling, is his business partner. Two of their joint businesses – Dice bar/restaurant and Dance Factory nightclub – also list a John David Owens as partner.*

Various sources indicate that the Atwals and Owens also control up to half of the door staff in Leicestershire. Owens has prior convictions – GBH, robbery, et cetera – so he can't work as a door attendant himself. However, he can and does supervise the staff he employs. He has been a model citizen for at least five years now, since his last stint in prison. He is forty-two years old and lives in Narborough. Bizarrely, he's also a paid-up member of three far-right-wing organizations.'

Amanda saw the shock on my face. How could she know so much, so quickly?

'It's amazing what you can find out on the Net,' she said, smiling at me. 'That's how you found Jennifer, isn't it?'

'What about the convictions and stuff – where they live? How'd you get that?'

'Journalists never reveal their sources,' she told me, her eyes glittering like sapphires. 'But I do have contacts in the police force – thanks to Jennifer.'

'The Atwals and Johnny Owens are well known,' added Jennifer. 'They've got a certain *reputation* around the city.'

I had a sudden flashback to DI Lucy Elliot's face. When I had given her Taz's name, she'd repeated it. At the time, I hadn't paid that much attention. Now, however, I realized that she already *knew* his name. That *had* to be it.

'Did you remember something?' asked Jennifer.

I nodded. 'When I reported Jas missing, the detective – I think she knew Taz . . .'

'Can you remember her name?'

'DI Elliot.'

'Lucy Elliot,' said Jennifer with a smile. 'I know her well.'

After some small talk, I told them all about Jas. I explained why I thought something was wrong. How she would never have run away. I also showed them the Facebook page and my other online efforts. The only thing I didn't speak about was the attack on me. I decided not to mention it. I had no proof of anything, no witnesses; just a very sore head.

After nearly an hour we stopped.

'Can I get you a sandwich or something?' asked Jennifer.

I said no but she ignored me.

'Young men need to eat,' she said sternly.

'What about the connection to Ricky?' I asked them both after lunch.

Jennifer looked through her notes before replying. 'It's the same person,' she told me. 'We did some checking, and Rajinder Athwal – with the "h" – owns a bar in Derby called Turpin's. He's listed at Companies House, with Taswinder Atwal, without the "h", as co-owner. So we know it's the same person. Somewhere along the line Ricky's name has been misspelt. Whether that was accidental or deliberate is debatable and not really very pertinent.'

I felt my stomach tighten. 'But isn't that *proof*?' I said. 'Ricky has a wife go missing and so does Taz. That can't be a coincidence, can it?'

Both women shook their heads.

'Common sense,' said Jennifer, 'tells us that it can't be coincidental. However, common sense isn't evidence or proof. Unless we have proof, we cannot accuse the Atwal brothers of anything. Legally thus far, it looks like a tragic coincidence. And if we print anything else, I'll be retiring sooner than I need to.'

'What about Dhaminder Singh?' I suggested. 'We could speak to him and get him involved with the story.'

Jennifer and Amanda looked at each other.

'What?' I wondered if something was wrong.

'We've already spoken to him,' admitted Jennifer. 'Yesterday, after you rang, I called him. He wanted to meet us today.'

'When?' I asked her.

'Er... he's arriving from Derby in twenty minutes... I hope that's OK with you, Sat,' she added.

'Yeah, that's fine. I wanted to meet him too.'

'Good,' replied Jennifer. 'I think the best approach

is a follow-up piece on Dhaminder and his sister. That way we can mention Jas's disappearance in the same light. Then we could get you to give us a quote, Sat. Is that what you were thinking when you mentioned Dhaminder?'

I nodded. 'Yeah – like, I could talk about understanding how he feels and all that stuff.'

Things were turning out well, but I was a little worried about meeting Dhaminder Singh. Not because he'd be a problem – that wasn't it. Mostly I was worried about my reaction to him. The more I learned about the Atwals, the more I realized that something awful had happened. It wasn't something I wanted to face. Meeting Dhaminder might force me to accept that Jas wasn't coming back. As I sat in that office and waited, I wondered if I was ready for that.

Four hours later, when we'd finished, I walked Dhaminder back to the train station. It was icy cold and the sky was the colour of slate. Little flecks of rain had begun to fall too. Dhaminder thanked me for getting in touch.

'It wasn't me,' I replied. 'Jennifer called you.'

He smiled at me as we stopped at a crossing opposite the station. 'Yeah,' he said, 'but you made the connection, didn't you?'

'I guess.'

Dhaminder Singh looked about Amar's age or maybe a little older. He had a long black beard and wore a tightly wrapped black turban. His skin was a creamy-white colour and his pale brown eyes were bright. He was big too, with broad shoulders and big thighs. Although he was no taller than me, he looked like he could pick me up with one hand.

'So, is anything else happening with your sister?' I asked him as the lights turned to red, stopping the traffic.

We crossed the ring road, then he turned to look at me. 'Not really,' he replied.

'It must be hard...' I trailed off, realizing immediately how stupid I sounded.

'You know how it feels, Sat.' Dhaminder's voice was full of sorrow.

'Yeah, I do.'

'After Anita disappeared we put up a reward for information about her, here and in India. Someone from over there contacted my family to say that they'd seen her, so I went over, but it was rubbish. They were just after the money. We've had a few like that over the last three years.'

Something inside forced me to ask my next question.

'Do you think that something *has* happened to her?' I asked. 'You know – something *bad*?'

Dhaminder sighed. 'I wish I could say that I believe

she's still alive – only I would be lying. If she was OK, she'd have contacted us by now. Lots of people talked when she disappeared. Most of them believed the Atwals. But there were also rumours that they'd hired people to kill her. And I believe *those* stories.'

My heart sank and I felt sick.

'We've tried everything,' he said. 'The police in Punjab looked for her, but they soon gave up. They didn't investigate the rumours about Ricky Atwal, even though I asked them to.'

'Why not?'

'Who knows? After that, I went to the police in Derby and they took the case on. Thing is, she went missing in India, and that was a problem. Our police had to go through the Indian authorities. There was no evidence and no body. So that's where things are – *nowhere*. My family are stuck in limbo. We don't know what to do or how we're supposed to feel. It's as though Anita just vanished into thin air.'

'So did Ricky live in Derby when he married Anita?' I was confused.

'Yeah – he left about a year after she disappeared,' Dhaminder told me. 'His dad was from Derby too. When Atwal senior went inside, the rest of the family moved to Leicester but Ricky kept the house in Derby. I think he still owns it.'

'What did Ricky's dad get done for?'

'Fraud and some other stuff. He's a nasty piece of work.'

'Did your family do the whole honour thing too?' I asked.

Dhaminder nodded. 'To begin with,' he said. 'They believed the Atwals, and my dad was angry as hell. But the more I pushed it, the more they came round.'

'I don't get it,' I said. 'I can't believe my family care more about their honour than they do about Jas.'

'There's a great wall of silence in our community when it comes to this stuff. They just want to ignore it. It's like *respect* means more to them.'

I sighed. 'It's hard. I can't stop thinking about Jas.'

'I wish I could say it gets better,' Dhaminder told me, 'but I don't want to lie to you.'

He gave me his mobile number and email address before heading off for the northbound platform. I stood and watched him leave, praying that he would find his sister one day, and hoping with all my heart that he was wrong about her being dead. If Anita Athwal *was* dead, then my chances of seeing Jas ever again were non-existent.

She stands by the washing machine, cold and fearful, looking at his back. He's stirring another spoonful of sugar into his tea; speaks without turning to face her.

'What was that?'

She wonders whether she should repeat herself. Wishes that she could summon up the courage.

'I ain't got all day,' he tells her. 'Speak up or piss off.'

She eyes the chef's knife nestling in the light-oak block, just out of reach. Longs to take it and push it through his heart, and look into his eyes as he dies. Just as he watched her when he stole her humanity away and left her with nothing inside. But she cannot bring herself to act. Despite everything he's done, he is a human being, and she cannot hurt him. Not physically. That would make her like him, and she refuses to plumb those depths.

'I want a divorce,' she hears herself say.

A snigger erupts from his mouth. He sets down the spoon and turns to face her. 'Are you for real?' he asks with a sneer.

She nods and looks into his bulging eyes, the pupils shiny and dilated, as cold as black granite.

'Never,' he replies.

'I don't c–c–care,' she stammers. 'I'm l-leaving.'

He considers her for a moment, and she knows that it is coming. The rage and the violence. She counts down to the explosion – reaches two, when he grabs her round the throat and lifts her off her feet. She struggles to breathe, eyes watering from the effort . . .

Yet, in her imagination, she is lying on a bed strewn with scarlet rose petals, her skin caressed by luxurious ivory-coloured silk. It is another man who stands at the foot of her bed, smiling warmly, his eyes glistening with love and pride. He comes to her, whispering words of adoration, and kisses her gently. Tells her of his pride at being her husband . . .

. . . her nose against the wall tiles. She can feel the bones breaking. Something pinches her side, tears away her flesh. He's taken her soul already, destroyed everything that makes her a woman. Anything else he takes matters little. She cannot breathe, cannot scream. She won't scream – won't give him that victory. Not any more.

'You think you're going to take what's mine?' he spits at her.

She wants to say that she will, wants to nod, but she cannot move.

'I'd rather kill you than let you take my money,' he says.

She feels herself go faint, knows that darkness is coming.

'You ever mention divorce again and I'll kill you, understand?'

She retreats into the only peace she has known since she married him. Unconsciousness . . .

Later, standing in the garden, cigarette in mouth, he calls his brother.

'She has to go,' he tells him. 'No way is she having my money.'

He listens to his brother's reply and takes the cigarette out of his mouth. Blue smoke curls around his features . . .

SIXTEEN

The story broke the following Monday. I got up early, skipped school and went to our newsagent's. I took two buses – one into the city centre, and then another to an area called Rushey Mead. My dad looked surprised to see me.

'Why aren't you at school?' he asked me in Punjabi.

'It's a study day,' I lied. 'Revision for the exams.'

My old man eyed me for a moment before shrugging.

'Do you want a cup of tea?' I asked as someone came in.

The shop was big, with four aisles down the middle and stock on three of the walls too. The newspapers and magazines were on the back wall, opposite the door, with the till to the left and a run of fridges to the right. There was another door in the rear left corner, which led into a back room. Dad had installed a small kitchen there, with a microwave, sink and worktop. Beyond that were shelves full of stock.

'In a minute,' my dad replied. 'Put some stuff out first.'

As I restocked the sweets, I watched him. First he tried to give a customer the wrong change; then he argued with some bloke over which cigarettes he'd asked for. He looked dishevelled: his cream turban was dirty and badly tied; his beige shirt and black trousers were creased, his face gaunt. The skin looked papery, especially under his eyes. The booze was taking its toll.

Once I'd finished sorting the sweets, I made the tea and brought a mug out to my dad. He was sitting at the counter, staring into space. I put the tea next to the till and asked if he was OK.

'Fine,' he muttered.

During my journey to the shop I had asked myself what I was doing. It made no sense to confront my dad – not when I knew that Jas's story would be in the paper. Only I wanted a chance to explain. I wanted to talk to him about Anita Athwal, about the similarities between her disappearance and my sister's. If he knew about Anita, he might listen to my suspicions. I knew that it might make things worse, but I *had* to try.

'I've been looking for information,' I told him.

'About what?' he asked without looking at me.

'Jas.'

He turned to me, shook his head. 'Why?'

'Because she's my sister – and *your* daughter. I *know* she didn't run away. Jas would never do that.'

Dad shook his head again. 'Taswinder showed us proof,' he insisted.

'I don't care.' I felt my annoyance growing. 'I don't

give a shit what Taz said. He means nothing to me. I only care about Jas.'

'You don't care?' My dad was getting agitated. 'Or maybe you don't understand? This is *shameful* for us. We can't even show our faces. Don't you *see* that?'

I sighed. 'That's rubbish! All that crap about honour and respect. What about *Jas*?'

'*She* did this!' shouted my dad. 'How many times must we tell you? Over and over again, the same bastard shit from your mouth!'

'But what if something happened to her?'

He gave me a strange look.

'What if Taz *did* something to her?'

'Taswinder did nothing. The sooner you realize that, the better.'

'I think he did,' I told my dad. 'And I think his family did it before too. A girl from Derby called Anita Athwal—'

He swore as another customer came through the door. It was an old Sikh man who stopped to chat with my dad. I went into the back, wondering how to convince my old man about Taz. It didn't matter anyway. The *Leicester Mercury* was due. Soon I would have to admit what I'd done.

I killed time checking sell-by dates. I found mouldy cheese, and milk that had expired before the weekend. It was obvious that Dad had lost interest. He was on autopilot, just taking money and making small talk. His mind was gone and he wasn't going to tell me where. I checked the rest of the fresh stock, removing greying sausages and cartons of juice turned sour. The *Leicester Mercury* arrived as I was getting rid of some seriously old bacon. My dad barely looked up, mumbling something to the driver and nodding towards the stand. The delivery man dropped the newspapers and left.

'You want me to sort them out?' I asked my dad.

He shrugged.

'Dad?'

'Why aren't you at school?' he asked me again.

'I already told you why.'

I looked at the front page, disappointed that it wasn't about Jas. Not that I'd expected it to be. The headline was about funding cuts in libraries across the city. I flicked the paper open and scanned through the pages. Jennifer Barton's story was on page eight. There was a big picture of Dhaminder standing in front of the *Mercury* building, holding a photograph of his sister. The story described his three-year search for information. As agreed, Jennifer had written about a fresh lead in Leicester, but without going into detail. The fresh lead was me, but she couldn't make that connection without evidence. A brief mention of Ricky Atwal claimed that the police had investigated him, before clearing his name.

My picture was below the main story, in a separate box. I was holding a photograph of my sister too. Beneath the picture, Jennifer had given some basic information about Jas. She'd also mentioned the link between Ricky and Taz – though without implying any wrongdoing. Finally there were details of my Facebook campaign. It wasn't much, but it was enough to get people thinking, enough to wind up the Atwals and enough to cause me more grief. I wondered how to tell my dad.

'You look after the shop,' he said to me suddenly. 'I need to go out.'

He didn't give me a chance to protest. He picked up his jacket, grunted something and left. I watched as he walked across the road and into a pub.

'Brilliant.'

Dad's mobile rang three times before I answered it. I found it under the counter, next to an aluminium rounders bat that he kept for protection. My brother's voice boomed out of the Nokia; he assumed that he was talking to my dad.

'Are you at the shop?' he asked in Punjabi.

'Er . . . it's me,' I replied.

Amar went quiet.

'Dad's in the pub,' I added.

'You staying there?' he asked, his voice stern.

157

'Well, I can't leave it, can I?' I said, looking around the empty shop.

'Ten minutes.' And Amar cut me off.

I put the phone back before tidying under the counter. The door opened with a *ping* and two lads, one Asian, one white, came in, heading straight for the drinks cooler. I looked out of the window towards the pub, ignoring them.

'Why i'n't the drinks cold?' the Asian one asked.

I turned to him and shrugged. 'Only just refilled the fridge,' I replied. 'They should be OK . . .'

The lad, a tall youth with dark wavy hair, shook his head. 'Warm, innit?'

I shrugged again and he came up to the counter.

'Ten Silk Cut too,' he said.

I shook my head. 'You ain't old enough,' I told him. 'One pound twenty for the drinks.'

He scowled, counted out the right change and threw it on the counter. 'Dickhead,' he muttered.

I looked from the change to the lad and shook my head again. 'Keep the money,' I told him. 'And get out.'

I could see the aggression in his face. I put my hand on the rounders bat, ready to smack him with it. I realized that I was angry with my dad and not those lads. I relaxed a little and took my hand off the bat.

'Leave it,' said the other boy, who was shaven-headed and wore a black Chelsea away shirt.

As we glared at each other, an old woman came in.

'Come!' said the white lad. 'Let's jet.'

The Asian gave me a dirty look, picked up his money and followed his friend out of the door, kicking the *Mercury* stand as he went.

'No manners nowadays,' said the woman, once the door had shut.

'Yeah,' I replied.

She spent five minutes talking nonsense and looking at stuff on the shelves before buying a tin of ravioli and some bread. Amar came in just as she was putting her change away.

'You drive fast,' I said, only he wasn't in the mood for jokes.

'Dad still in the pub?' he asked, eyeing the pile of *Mercury*s sitting on the counter.

I nodded. 'You seen it, then?' My question was redundant. It was obvious that he had.

Amar ignored me; he walked round the counter and stopped in front of me. 'Are you thick?' he asked me quietly.

I shook my head.

'*No?*' he spat, his voice rising. 'You *absolutely* sure about that?'

I stepped back, thinking he was going to punch me.

'I've already had three phone calls since the paper came out,' he told me. '*Three.*'

'I wanted to—' I began.

Amar's right hand shot out and gripped me around the throat. He pushed me back so that my head was pressed against the shop window. 'Shut up!' he warned.

I tried to break free but he was too strong for me. His grip was vice-like.

'Gerroff!' I managed to get out. I felt angry and scared and humiliated.

'Everyone is gonna see it,' he told me. '*Everyone.*'

I saw his eyes shift from my face to something in the street. He let me go. I rubbed my neck, fighting the urge to punch him. The door pinged again, revealing my dad. He was holding a rolled-up copy of the *Mercury*. His face was red and his eyes were on fire. He threw the newspaper at my head.

'*Stupid bastard!*' he yelled, lunging towards the counter.

I fell back, catching my head on the cigarette display.

'*Leave him alone!*' I heard Amar shout.

Dad punched the till before pushing everything off the counter. Newspapers, sweets and stationery went flying, just as two teenage girls walked in. They took one look and turned away, giggling as they left.

Amar locked the door behind them. 'In the back!' he ordered.

'No,' I replied. 'You got summat to say, you do it here.'

'*Shut your mouth!*' shouted my dad.

'In the back – *now!*' Amar repeated.

I grabbed the rounders bat and held it up. 'You touch me again,' I told my brother, 'and I'm gonna lamp you with this, you get me?'

He watched Dad go into the stockroom and seemed to calm down. 'Put that thing away,' he said. 'No one is gonna hit you.'

'Yeah – so why grab me then?'

'Because I was angry, Sat.' He looked ashamed. 'I didn't mean to hurt you. Honest . . .'

I waited a few seconds, trying to calm down and catch my breath. Allowing time for Dad to cool down too. Eventually I followed Amar into the back. My old man was cracking open a bottle of Bell's. He washed out two mugs and poured a large shot in each. He handed one to my brother, and took a swig of his own. Amar looked at me and shook his head.

'Why?' he asked.

I poured myself a shot of whisky too. Neither of them blinked as I took a swig, struggling not to hurl as it burned my throat.

'Sat . . . ?'

I waited until my stomach had settled before replying. 'Because you don't give a shit!'

Amar frowned. 'Of course we *care*. But we can't change what happened.'

'You don't *know* what happened,' I pointed out. 'You

just believed everything Taz told you.'

My dad gulped down his whisky, then poured some more.

'We've *seen* the proof,' argued Amar for the umpteenth time. 'Are you saying Taz made that up – all those disgusting messages?'

I shrugged. 'Did you read the article about Anita Athwal?' I asked. 'Did you even *look* at it?'

Amar sighed. 'It's nothing to do with us.'

'Don't you think it's weird, though? Two women missing from the same family?'

'The police looked into the first case and found nothing. There's no link and no evidence. It's just a coincidence. All you've done is embarrass everyone.'

It was my turn to sigh. '*Embarrass?*' I asked. 'Is that all you care about?'

Amar looked at Dad. 'You might not care about our reputation, but we do. Everyone in Leicester will know now. You think that's good? Mum and Dad get funny looks everywhere they go. People are gossiping. And you're making it worse. All 'cos you can't accept the truth and keep your mouth shut.'

There was little point in arguing again – going over and over the same points. It didn't matter what the article said. Amar wasn't going to change his mind.

'You didn't see *all* the evidence,' he continued. 'Otherwise you'd understand. Some of them messages

162

made me feel sick. Stuff that the *worst* kind of slag wouldn't say.'

'Jas ain't no slag!' I shouted, my temper flaring up again.

'So why the affair then? Why did she send them nasty messages to a Paki?'

'I don't know,' I admitted. 'But it wasn't Jas. I just know it wasn't.'

Dad slammed his mug down on the worktop. *'Enough!'* he shouted at both of us.

'But—' I began.

'Nothing!' he yelled in Punjabi. 'You know *nothing*. I saw the proof – things no father should have to see. That girl has ruined my reputation. She means nothing to me now – understand? Not a thing.'

Amar's ring tone, a classic bhangra tune, sounded. He ignored it until it stopped. When it rang a second time, he pulled out his Samsung and answered impatiently. *'Yeah?'*

I watched as his anger faded, replaced by concern.

'Which hospital?' he asked quietly.

Someone was talking frantically on the other end of the line.

'On my way.' Amar ended the call.

'What is it?' I asked.

He gulped down air. 'It's Mandy,' he said. 'There's something wrong with the baby . . .'

Laura watched Johnny Owens swagger across the empty bar and into the office as she finished a stock check. He was wearing his golfing outfit — a red and green checked polo shirt that strained across his massive back, black trousers and two-tone black and white shoes. On his head was a flat cap he'd managed to find in an almost identical check to his polo shirt. He looked ridiculous, but not many people were brave enough to say so. Taz and Ricky were waiting for him — both in foul moods, which was hardly surprising. One of the bar staff, a student called Cerys, had shown Laura the previous day's article.

Now Laura was desperate to know what Taz and Ricky would say. The story had come as a shock. She thought back to a rainy afternoon the previous summer, when Taz had encouraged her to play a trick on his wife; asked Laura to set up email accounts in her name and send explicit messages to another fake account. Explicit messages that he had dreamed up with Laura — high on coke and half a bottle of Jack

Daniel's. The thought that those fake messages had caused such problems made her feel ill.

'Cerys?' she called.

A young woman poked her head up from behind the bar. She was short, with long curly black hair, sparkling honey-coloured eyes and curves that made Laura feel like a little boy in comparison.

'Yeah?' she asked in her singsong Scouse accent.

'We need to stock up Corona, Beck's and Bulmers, and then look at the spirits.'

'Will do,' Cerys replied with a big smile.

'And put those boobs away,' joked Laura. 'I'm getting jealous.'

Cerys grinned. 'They say more than a handful's a waste – but I've never had any complaints!'

'I bet,' said Laura, grinning back at her.

She watched as Cerys turned to the glass-doored fridges behind the bar, her top riding up to show the tattoo in the small of her back.

'Put the bum away too,' Laura told her.

She turned and headed for the office, which lay behind the bar. It was down a narrow corridor that led to the rear fire exit. The door was only slightly ajar, but it was enough for Laura to hear everything. She leaned back against the wall and listened . . .

* * *

Taz clenched the blue stapler in his left hand, the veins ready to pop through his skin. His head pounded and his heart was beating fast.

'When are the coppers coming?' asked Ricky.

'They should be here any time,' he replied, slamming the stapler down on his desk.

'And?'

Taz gave his brother a hard look. 'And what, you dickhead?' he spat out. 'I'll deal with it.'

Johnny Owens leaned against Ricky's desk and sniffed. 'You want me to do the kid again?' he asked.

Taz shook his head and brushed lint off his light grey Hugo Boss suit. 'Not yet.'

'Why not?'

'Give it a few days,' said Taz. 'You know the police are gonna get hype . . .'

Johnny shrugged. 'You handle them,' he suggested. 'Me and Ricky will deal with the kid—'

'And his family,' said Ricky, reaching across his desk for a silver cigarette case.

'Shit,' said Taz. 'This is all we need.'

Johnny and Ricky looked at each other, thinking the same thing. The brothers were in the middle of a dispute. The owner of a rival firm that provided door staff, Lucas Marks, was making trouble and things were getting hot. They didn't need police attention because of some snivelling kid.

'Tiger Woods over here is right,' said Ricky.

'I ain't no monkey,' protested Johnny.

'You're dressed like one,' joked Ricky, lighting a fag and replacing the cigarette case.

'I need a line,' said Taz.

Ricky grinned at his brother and got out his cocaine. The lining of his royal blue Ted Baker suit matched the colour of the cigarette case.

'You heard anything else from Lucas Marks?' Johnny asked Taz.

'He ain't shit,' he replied. 'He ain't got enough staff to take our doors.'

'But he's sniffing around?'

'Yeah, but not for long.'

Johnny clenched and unclenched his giant fists. 'Ain't no one taking bread outta my pockets,' he warned.

'Exactly, Johnny. We've worked too hard to get here and we're gonna expand.'

'Not if we're in prison,' Ricky pointed out.

'Enough pissing about,' said Johnny. 'The kid gets sorted first, and then Lucas. Soon as.'

Taz shrugged.

'So what you gonna tell the coppers?' asked Ricky, rolling up a fifty-pound note.

'Same as before,' Taz told his brother. 'No evidence then, and none now, bro. What they gonna do – invent some?'

Johnny grinned at both of them. 'They'll have a job,' he said. 'There wasn't anything left anyway.'

Taz went over to Ricky's desk, took the note and hoovered up a fat line of white powder.

'End of the week,' said Ricky, lighting another fag.

'Ready when yer ready,' replied Johnny.

Laura jumped when she felt the hand on her back. 'Shit!'

She turned to find an apologetic Cerys standing behind her, wide-eyed.

'I'm sorry – I didn't mean to—' Cerys began.

'It's OK,' interrupted Laura. 'I just didn't hear you.'

'There's some police officers out the front,' said Cerys.

'All right. I'll let Taz know.'

Laura waited for Cerys to go before knocking on the office door.

'Yeah?!' Taz shouted.

She pushed the door open. 'The police are here,'

she told him, hoping that her face wouldn't give her away.

'How long you been standing there?' asked a suspicious-looking Ricky.

'I haven't,' she lied. 'How long have you been a prick?'

'Leave it,' said Taz as Ricky started to react.

'Big mouth you've got,' his brother said, glaring at Laura.

Laura ignored him and asked Taz what was going on.

'Trouble,' he replied. 'Summat to do with the door from the other day . . .'

Laura nodded. 'I must have missed it,' she said, angry to see how easily lies came to Taz.

'Your night off,' added Johnny. 'You would have been home, doing your nails or whatever.'

Laura asked Taz what to tell the police.

'Nuttin', babe,' he said. 'I'm coming out.'

Ricky looked down at his desk. 'Ask 'em if they fancy a toot,' he joked.

Taz shook his head, and followed Laura back into the bar.

Once they were gone Johnny turned to Ricky.

'The kid didn't get the message,' he said.

Ricky nodded. 'I know that, Johnny.'

'Just saying. Time to scare him again – properly this time. I'll handle it.'

'You and me both,' said Ricky.

After speaking to the police officers, Laura told Taz that she was leaving for the day. When he protested, she lied about having period pains. Taz grimaced and said whatever.

'I'm gonna take a few days off,' she told him.

'A few days?'

Laura nodded, wondering whether he'd argue the toss. 'My mum's ill,' she lied again.

Taz was glancing at the police. Distracted. He barely heard her reply. 'OK – I'll call you later,' he said without looking at her.

'Don't,' replied Laura. 'I'll call you.'

'Whatever.'

The drive home took ten minutes. Once she was through the door, Laura collapsed onto the sofa. She thought about everything she'd overheard – everything she had learned about Taz. About the lies she'd been told and those she'd helped to create. She recalled a strange conversation with Johnny Owens – dismissed as yet another bullshit story.

171

'That's me in Thailand,' he'd bragged, showing Laura his phone. 'That's one of them big temples an' that . . .'

'But that's not in Thailand,' Laura had pointed out.

'Course it is,' he'd said. 'I was there, love, not you.'

At the time, Laura had laughed and walked away. Now that she knew better, however, she felt sick.

Finally she found herself picturing two young women: happy, pretty girls she'd never met yet felt she knew. As Laura pondered those young girls, she felt torrents of bile forcing their way up into her mouth. She ran for the bathroom, tears of anger and guilt working their way down her face.

SEVENTEEN

After explaining what had happened, Amar rushed to the hospital. The doctor had admitted Mandy because her high blood pressure was affecting the baby. They wanted to keep her in so that they could monitor things. Dad closed up as soon as Amar left before calling a relative.

'Uncle Binny will take care of the shop,' he told me. 'He has a set of keys. We need to get home and pick up your mother.'

I nodded, grabbing a copy of the *Mercury* on my way out. My dad drove like a nutter, weaving through the traffic back to Oadby. He didn't even turn off the engine once we got home. He just stayed there, the engine purring on the driveway.

'Get your mother – *hurry*,' he said to me. 'And you stay home in case the phone rings.'

I gave him a look. 'I want to come,' I insisted. 'Besides, who's gonna call?'

Dad shook his head. 'Satinder,' he said firmly, 'for once in your life, you listen. *Please?*'

Mum was already at the door, fretting. 'What's happening?' she asked me, her eyes wide with shock. 'Amar just said to wait for you.'

173

'Mandy's ill,' I explained. 'Amar went to the hospital and Dad's taking you too.'

'Oh God!' she cried.

'It's OK, Mum,' I said, giving her a hug. 'The doctors will take care of them.'

My mum mumbled something about food in the kitchen and tea on the cooker.

I told her to forget it. 'I'm staying at home,' I said. 'Don't worry about the house. Just go.'

She ran her fingers down my left cheek. 'You can be a good boy sometimes, Satinder,' she told me.

'Mum!'

'If anyone calls,' she added, 'don't tell them anything. You know how these people talk.'

Dad beeped the horn impatiently and I edged her towards the car. As they drove away, I looked down at the newspaper that was still in my hands, sighed and went indoors.

Amar called me around five. Mandy and the unborn baby were stable, but the doctors were worried about complications. They had done various tests and were waiting on the results.

'We won't be back until we know,' he told me.

'That's OK,' I replied. 'I'm here.'

'Has anyone called?'

'Just Uncle Binny. I told him I didn't know anything,' I said.

'Is he OK running the shop?'

'Yeah. He said he can open up tomorrow too, if you need him.'

'Yeah,' said Amar. 'I'll call him now.'

Mandy stayed in hospital the next night too, and once again I was all alone. I ordered a greasy pizza, regretting it as I watched *EastEnders*. I was on my third can of Coke Zero when the doorbell rang. Thinking that it might be a relative, I put down the drink, belched and opened the door. A white bloke stood on the doorstep, smiling at me. He was short and wide and wore a black suit, his white shirt unbuttoned at the collar, and shiny, pointed black shoes. He had fair, cropped hair and a small red crescent ran from his left eye onto his cheek.

'Evening, sir.' He asked me how many windows I wanted to replace.

I sighed, then said dismissively, 'I don't own the house.'

'Yes,' he said, his expression unchanging, 'but you *do* live here, don't yer?'

'Yeah – I just opened the door, didn't I?'

The man continued to smile but his eyes went cold. 'So,' he said, 'how many of yer fucking windows do yer want replacing?'

His words didn't register for a second, but when they finally made sense, my stomach lurched. I tried to shut the door on him, but he stopped me, using his upper-body strength and huge hands.

'I could do yer three, maybe four,' he said. 'Only I'd have to break the bastards first . . .'

I was scared but didn't want to show it. *'Get off my drive!'* I shouted, hoping that the neighbours would hear.

'Make me,' replied the man, sneering at me.

'I'm gonna call the police,' I warned.

'What?' he asked, pulling a blade from his jacket. 'You gonna reach the phone before I reach you?'

I thought about it for a second. He was right. As soon as I tried, he'd jump me.

'What do you want?' I asked, my voice beginning to betray me. The knife had a serrated edge, the teeth sharp.

'There, there,' he replied, brandishing his weapon. 'That's better, isn't it, Mr Kooner.'

An ice-cold finger worked its way down my back. I realized that he was here about the *Mercury* article.

'Taz sent you,' I said.

'No more talking,' the man warned. 'Keep your mouth *shut*. Understand?'

I nodded.

'Do you un-der-stand?' he repeated slowly, stabbing the knife in my direction, emphasizing each syllable.

'I understand,' I told him, my eyes never leaving the blade.

'Good,' he replied. 'Next time I'll cut out yer eyes and feed 'em to yer.'

With that, he turned and walked back down the drive. I watched him go, relief spreading through my body. Relief mixed with anger. I thought about ringing my brother but decided against it. Amar had enough problems of his own at the moment.

Back in the living room, I found myself scrolling through my phone's contacts list, stopping when I reached Taz's number. My head was ready to explode. I knew that calling him would be stupid, but I still held my phone ready. I pressed the 'call' button, listening as it went straight to answerphone. The grease from the pizza was making my stomach churn. For a moment I thought I was going to puke, but I managed to stop myself. I composed myself and spoke into the phone.

'Taz – it's Sat. I've just had your mate round. You can do what you like but I'm gonna get you! Do you understand? I'm gonna get you for what you did to Jas, you fucking prick! The next time you send someone round my house I'm gonna come for you – you get me? *Fuck off!*'

My family returned just before midnight. Amar and Dad headed straight for the drinks cabinet, settling down in the living room. My mum found me in the kitchen, browsing Amazon on the family laptop. I tried to stay

177

calm so that she wouldn't realize I was scared.

'How's Mandy?' I asked her as I clicked on a link.

Mum sat at the table, yawning. 'She's stable,' she replied eventually in Punjabi. 'More tests tomorrow.'

I looked up. 'Is the baby OK?'

'Yes.'

I looked at the iPod I had up on the screen, checking its capacity. I wondered whether to speak to Amar about Taz's warning, but decided against it. It could wait until Mandy and the baby were out of danger.

'Your dad told me,' Mum went on.

I looked up at her, wondering if she could read my mind.

'The newspaper,' she said, eyeing the kitchen door, which stood wide open. She got up and switched the kettle on before padding over to the door in her slippers and shutting it.

'Oh . . . that,' I replied.

'I don't understand you,' she said, returning to the table.

'I don't understand you either,' I told her. 'All this anger towards Jas.'

Sadness crept across her face and she lowered her eyes. 'I'm not angry, *beteh*,' she said. 'Not like that.'

I glared at her. 'Not angry?' I snapped. 'So why aren't you talking about Jas?'

'What am I supposed to say?' she asked me. 'Your

father won't listen – not to anyone. He is hurt.'

'What's the point in talking?' I said. 'I'm going round in circles. Do you know how many times I've tried to speak to Dad and Amar? They say the same thing every time.'

'Why did you speak to the newspaper people?'

'Because it was my last chance. No one else cares – only me . . . I had to do something.'

Mum shook her head. '*I* care,' she told me. 'We all do. Jas is our daughter, *beteh*. She is part of us, just like you and Amar. No matter what he tells you, your father loves that girl.'

I snorted. 'Not enough to take her side,' I said. 'He'd rather listen to Taz.'

My mum considered me for a moment before replying. 'And what has Taz done?' she asked.

I told her all about Anita Athwal and her brother's search. As I did so, her eyes grew wide. I could see the hope in her expression.

'But if this is true, why didn't the police arrest them?' she asked when I was done.

I shrugged. 'Not enough evidence.'

'But that could mean they are innocent.'

'*No!*' I shouted. '*Jas* is innocent; Anita too. How can you even *think* that?'

'But what have they done?' she asked me. 'What proof do you have?'

I thought back to the pub, and to the thug at the

door. I wanted to tell her, to show her that Taz was hiding something. Only I couldn't. I didn't want to frighten her or create more stress. She was scared stiff about Mandy and the baby – I could see that. I shook my head at her, realizing that I was on my own. I was the only one who really cared about my sister, and that hurt. I looked at my mum, and pushed the laptop away.

'You know what Jas is like,' I said. 'Everyone knows. She would never have done this. *That's* how I know about Taz.'

'I don't understand,' she replied. 'He showed the proof to Amar. She ran off with that Muslim boy. Everyone knows it.'

'I *know* about Taz because I *trust* my sister,' I explained. 'I know her better than you or anyone. I'm the *only* one who believes in her. And no one will ever take that away.'

Mum stood up, ignoring the boiling kettle. She looked at me wearily. 'This is no good,' she said. 'You are embarrassing us in public. I know you're upset, but this is wrong.'

'You, Dad, Amar – you're all the same!' I said angrily. 'It's all about protecting your bloody honour. Not love, not Jas and not me – just *izzat*. But all you're doing is killing it – killing honour – not defending it!'

'Don't speak to me like that,' she warned, her face

growing stern.

'I don't care any more,' I told her. 'As soon as I can, I'm out of here. You can keep your stupid views about honour. I'm gonna find out what happened to Jas without you – any of you!'

She sighed and shook her head. 'One day you'll understand,' she said softly.

She turned and left me to brood on my own.

EIGHTEEN

My nephew was born the same night, just after three
a.m. After all the worry, he was fine. I saw him the
following evening. He was tiny, wrinkly and smelled
of milk. His eyes were dark blue and he had a full
head of jet-black hair. When I looked into his cot, I
was shocked at the size of his hands and feet. They
seemed too small, even for a baby. Mandy, who was
much better, laughed when she saw me staring.

'He won't break,' she told me, more than once. 'Pick
him up. We're gonna call him Aran.'

My parents wanted to arrange a blessing for him.
They decided to avoid the *gurdwara* and have it at
home. I overheard Amar and Mandy talking about it. My
parents were convinced that people were gossiping,
slagging them off. I heard Amar say that the shame
was still eating away at them. I got angry listening to
them, but I knew I couldn't react. If I did, they'd just be
stressed. They wouldn't listen to my concerns about
Jas. I had no choice – I had to pretend not to care.

Over the following week I found the silence hard to
take. I started spending too much time in my room,
glued to the PC or just sitting in darkness. I joined my
dad in the evenings, throwing down shots of Chivas

Regal like they were water. My dad loved it, thought I was wetting the baby's head. He even gave me a load of cash, telling me to treat myself.

'You are an uncle for the first time,' he said to me. 'You've been blessed.'

I wanted to ask him about Aran's aunt, my sister, but I didn't. As I told myself repeatedly, there was no point. Aran's arrival had pushed Jas even further out of the picture. It was as though he had filled the hole she'd made when she vanished. At least, it did for the rest of them.

Dash was busy with revision all through the holidays; Charlotte too. I sent her a text about Aran, and she seemed excited and happy, but I didn't go round. I wanted to tell her what was going on, confide in her, but I couldn't. She'd made it clear that she needed space. Instead, I sat and sulked on my own, getting more and more depressed. The letter from school arrived too. It explained that I'd been temporarily excluded for unexplained absences until my parents contacted the assistant principal. I wasn't shocked – I'd been expecting it, but that didn't help my mood. It was just another load on an ever-increasing pile of shit. Amar and Dad didn't care. When I told them, they just shrugged at me.

'You've had a lot on your mind,' my dad said.

'If you mess up this year, you can go back next year,'

added Amar. 'They can't blame you for what happened to Aran. It's understandable.'

I remember wanting to shout at him. It had nothing to do with Aran – it was all about my sister. Only I didn't shout – I didn't see the point.

The following night, as I walked back from Asda, a silver Mercedes passed by, splashing through the heavy rain. At the end of the road, at the mini-roundabout, it turned and came back on itself. I stopped, still paranoid about the attacks and ready to run, but the car didn't stop. The driver was a black man with a head like a cannonball. He wore sunglasses despite the darkness. The car disappeared around a corner and I set off again, praying that it wouldn't return.

At the junction of my road I sped up, my heart drumming against the wall of my chest. Three houses from mine, I heard brakes screeching. A car door opened and closed. I turned, coming face to face with the Mercedes driver. I got out my keys, pushing one through the middle fingers on my right hand. If the man tried anything, I would bury the key in his head.

'What?' I asked.

The man stayed where he was and removed his sunglasses. He was huge; a stereotypical gangster in a long black coat that looked like it might rip at any second. His face was long and horsey. His jaw matched his shoulders and chest – strong and powerful. As I watched him, the passenger door opened. Ricky Atwal got out. He was wearing silver track pants, blue and white Nike Airs and a steel-grey hooded top. I felt my legs turn to jelly as I looked around frantically.

'Easy, Sat.' He grinned at me. The skin around his eyes was dark and baggy – as though he hadn't slept for a week.

'What?' I repeated, hoping to see a neighbour. The rain was intense; the street deserted. I was on my own.

'Easy, bro,' Ricky sneered. 'Always good to catch up with the family.'

I shook my head. 'You ain't my family.'

I felt myself grow tense as the driver took a step towards me.

'What's with the stupid message?' asked Ricky. 'You upset Taz . . .'

'So?'

'Not very nice, is it? He done your sister – you should show some respect.'

I clenched my fists, started to move, forgetting to be scared. I wanted to kill Ricky for what he'd said.

'I wouldn't do that,' he warned. 'My friend won't like it.'

I tried to calm down and took a step backwards, wondering if I should just run. Only there was nowhere to go.

'He can do some serious damage,' Ricky went on. 'Just one word, Sat – all it would take.'

'Bring it, then,' I spat, praying that he wouldn't see how scared I was. It didn't work.

'You're shaking, mate. Are you shitting it?'

I shook my head slowly, my eyes never leaving the driver.

'One word,' repeated Ricky. 'Any *time*, any *place* . . .'

'What do you want?'

'You *know* what I want. Last chance.'

I nodded – I didn't know what else to do.

'No more newspapers, no more coppers . . . We don't *like* being disturbed,' said Ricky. 'See, if it comes down to it, what have you got, really?'

He paused and looked at the driver. Then he drew out a silver handgun. 'You wanna disrespect *us*?' he continued, pointing the weapon at me. My legs began to shake and butterflies fluttered in my bowel. A single bubble of air rose up my gullet.

'I'll keep quiet,' I said.

Ricky ignored me. 'Think you can cause us trouble? The world don't work that way, Sat. We decide and you follow. That goes for *all* of you Kooners. Shame your dirty bitch sister never understood that . . .'

I wanted to kill him, but I just stood there, fighting back tears of frustration and anger. I was stuck. I couldn't do a thing. Attacking Ricky would be crazy.

He would kill me. I was useless, insignificant, and so was my sister. That was the reality. The Atwals could do what they liked. People like my family couldn't stand up to them. They were too strong. All these thoughts flooded through my brain as I stood in the rain, facing Ricky and his driver.

'Last chance,' repeated Ricky. 'Next time you won't see us coming. Not you, not your family . . .'

'I understand,' I replied, my head feeling light.

'Hope so.' He put the gun away. 'I hate killing people. Messes with my high, you get me? I always liked your dad too. Hurting him would be wrong.'

I nodded and watched them leave, wondering what to do. The rain had soaked me to the bone but I didn't move. I just stood there, thinking. Each time I came to the same conclusion: nothing. I could do nothing. The Atwals had beaten me, and my family didn't care. I was truly alone.

Meeting Laura a couple of weeks later seemed like an accident. I was out drinking on my own in some bar called Chilli. I was angry and depressed, feeling useless. All I wanted to do was forget about things for one night. Just one night when my mind wasn't filled with thoughts of Jas. I bumped into some lads I knew, Pete and Surj. They were from rich Punjabi families and spent their time getting drunk, listening to bhangra and chasing girls. Normally I would have avoided them, but I couldn't that night. They bought me a load of drinks and asked about people we knew in common. I didn't want to be rude so I joined them. Soon we were all drunk and they started getting rowdy.

I was at the bar, buying sambuca shooters, when Pete and Surj kicked off behind me. I turned round to see Pete butting some Asian lad, whose girl started screaming. Two more lads, both white, jumped Pete as Surj threw wild punches. The bouncers were in quickly, dragging Pete and Surj away and throwing them out. When I tried to follow, the Asian boy that Pete had smacked blocked my path.

'He's with 'em,' he said to his mates.

Suddenly a group of white and Asian lads had surrounded me. I looked around for the bouncers, but they were busy at the door. Realizing that I was in trouble, I started to panic. I was going to get battered. That was when Laura stepped in. I didn't recognize her – that came a bit later – and I thought it was strange that some random girl was trying to help, but I was pleased to see her anyway. She spoke to the Asian lad, who was about six feet tall, with wavy chestnut hair and broad shoulders, nodding in my direction. He shook his head. I watched as she said something else. This time he shrugged.

Laura turned to me. 'Come on,' she said.

'Huh?'

'Time to leave.'

'But how did you . . . ?'

Laura grinned at me. 'They're all friends with my baby brother,' she revealed. 'But we should still go . . .'

The gang didn't look pleased. Realizing that Laura was right, I followed her. Out on the street, I couldn't see Pete or Surj anywhere. I turned to Laura and thanked her.

'No problem,' she said. 'I hate stuff like that.'

'But you don't even know me,' I replied.

Laura smiled. 'You don't remember me then?'

I looked at her and tried to think. My brain wasn't processing at full speed. It was on Jack Daniel's and sambuca time. She was an inch taller than I was, with short, almost black hair, pale skin with pink cheeks, full lips and light hazel eyes. She wore no make-up at all and her black dress was tight, hugging a slim figure. She was carrying a small black bag, and instead of fancy shoes, she had bright white trainers on her feet. She was well cute.

'Er . . . no.' I tried not to stare at her.

'What if I was holding a clipboard?'

That was when I got it. 'Shit!' I said without thinking.

'Well, I've had better reactions,' she replied, smiling at me.

'You work at Dice,' I said as paranoia struck.

She shook her head. 'Not any more.'

I looked into her eyes, trying to work out if she was lying to me. To see if I was being set up by Taz.

'I left a couple of weeks ago. I'm Laura.'

I relaxed a little when I saw how genuine she was. Being gorgeous didn't harm her cause either. 'Sat,' I replied.

Laura asked me if I wanted to get a drink somewhere else.

'I was gonna head home,' I told her, instantly regretting my reply.

'Oh,' she said, sounding a bit annoyed.

'I *was*,' I said quickly, warming to the idea of spending time with a fit older woman. 'I thought I was too young, anyway,' I added. 'That's what you said at New Year's.'

Laura laughed out loud. 'You don't look like a kid – well, not any more . . . Besides, I'm only twenty-one myself. I'm not exactly some grand old dame, am I?'

'I'm surprised that you remembered me,' I replied. 'That was months ago.'

She shrugged, looking away for a moment. 'I'm good with faces,' she told me. 'I won't remember your name tomorrow but I'll never forget your face. Helps me keep idiots out of the bar – or at least it *did*.'

This time I laughed. 'Sounds useful to me,' I said. 'Where we going – Dice?'

Laura shook her head. 'I don't like it in there. Never have.'

'Well, I'm barred anyway,' I told her. 'Me and Taz had a problem.'

She looked at me funny – or so it seemed at the time. 'Taz is related to you, isn't he? Brother-in-law,' she said.

I nodded. 'It's a long story . . .' I wondered how to explain without giving too much away. 'We don't get on – family trouble.'

'That Asian thing?' Laura asked. 'I never got that.'

'What's that?'

'Family,' she said. 'There were always people turning up claiming to be cousins or summat.'

'Not me,' I said. 'Not any more.'

'What – you just *stopped* being family?' Laura stared into my eyes with such intensity that I had to look away.

'Summat like that,' I replied. 'Anyway, I don't wanna talk about it. I get pissed off. We having a drink or what?'

Laura nodded and told me we were getting a cab.

'Where to?' I asked, feeling a pinch of guilt over Charlotte. Only I wasn't the one who'd asked for space. What was I supposed to do? I asked myself. Stop going out?

'Clarendon Park,' said Laura, breaking into my thoughts. 'I hate town – full of dickheads.'

'Good job I've got cash then,' I told her.

'Ooh,' she joked. 'Young and rich. Lucky me!'

Amanda asked me if I wanted another coffee. I shook my head.

'What do you want to do?'

I looked out of her living-room window, watching the sky turn a blue-grey shade as automated timers began to switch on the streetlights.

'About what?'

'This is taking a long time,' she replied. 'Is there much more?'

I nodded.

'Do you know what time the last train back to Leicester is?'

I shrugged. I wasn't sure whether to tell her the truth: that I was safer staying away from Leicester.

'Does it matter?' I asked. 'If I miss it, I can always call my mate and see if I can crash there.'

'OK,' Amanda said. 'So let me get this right . . . You called the police and they took no notice because there was no evidence of any wrongdoing. Then you found out about

Anita Athwal and contacted Jennifer?'

'And you,' I said.

'I'm sorry?'

'You and Jennifer.'

'Oh yeah.' Amanda smiled at me. 'We revisited the story about Anita and mentioned your sister at the bottom. Ricky and Taz Atwal saw it and threatened you.'

'Yes,' I replied. 'And my family went mad too.'

'And you didn't go to the police about the threats or getting attacked,' she continued.

'No — I was too scared. I thought they'd hurt my family.'

'And not even your brother believed you about Jas?' she asked.

I shook my head. 'No. He took Taz's word as the truth. All the emails and texts and stuff that Taz showed him. He didn't even mention Jas by name . . . none of them did. It was like she was dead to them.'

'Honour,' Amanda murmured quietly.

'Honour,' I repeated, wondering how such a small word could have caused so much trouble.

'I'm hungry,' she said suddenly. 'Fancy some food?'

I shrugged again.

'There's a really good Sri Lankan place on the corner.'

She nodded towards the window. 'I'll order and we can pick it up.'

'OK,' I said. 'I've got some money . . .'

Amanda gave me a funny look, her eyes boring into mine, making me feel uncomfortable. I turned away.

'I'm sure I can stretch to some fried fish and rice,' she said in her throaty voice.

'Where are you from?' I asked.

'Why?'

'You ain't got an accent,' I said. 'It sounds a bit London, but then it goes somewhere else . . .'

'Lewisham,' she replied. 'I lived there until I was eighteen and then I went to uni in Sheffield.'

'So how'd you end up at the *Leicester Mercury*?' I stood up and stretched my legs by walking over to the window. The street was full of people wandering in and out of bars and restaurants. It looked like a cool place to live.

'Saw an advert. Applied, met Jennifer and that's it.'

'Fried fish?' I said as I watched a sky-blue taxi pull up outside an old-fashioned pub called The Lion.

'It's bloody amazing,' said Amanda, going over to a small wooden table and picking up a takeaway menu. She handed it to me before turning on a standard lamp.

One corner of the room was suddenly lit up in a deep orange glow.

As I looked at the menu, Amanda started to re-read her notes. After a few minutes she turned back to me.

'So?' she asked.

'Huh?'

'Fried fish or something else?'

I told her what I wanted and watched her pick up her iPhone. As she put in the order, I thought back to what had happened after I met Laura. Back to the shock I'd felt when I found out who she was.

Amanda asked me about Laura as we sat down to eat. I was busy looking at my food, wondering whether I was supposed to eat the fried fish whole or maybe cut the heads off.

'She was Taz's girlfriend,' I replied, unable to tear my gaze away from the fish heads.

'I'm sorry?' she replied, the shock evident in her voice.

'That's exactly what I did when she told me,' I said. 'Laura was Taz's girlfriend all the way through his marriage to my sister. And for a long time before that . . .'

Amanda put down the piece of naan she was holding.

'She knows all about Anita too,' I added. 'She was with Taz when Anita married Ricky.'

'So she's the witness you told me about earlier?'

'Yeah. She told me loads of stuff. About the emails that Jas was supposed to have sent. All them text messages and stuff — the Facebook page? Laura and Taz made all that up.'

Amanda's eyes widened. 'So why didn't you go straight to the police?' she asked.

'It's complicated,' I replied. 'Someone saw us together and told Taz . . .'

'Oh,' said Amanda.

'Then Laura disappeared too.'

NINETEEN

I was looking through Laura's CD and book collection when I saw the newspaper. I nearly missed it – tucked away between Levi Roots' *Reggae Reggae Cookbook* and a James Lee Burke novel called *Burning Angel*.

It was two weeks after we met. We had spent a few nights together, going out and getting drunk. On other evenings we'd sit in her flat on Queens Road, watching DVDs. There was nothing in it – nothing sexual, even though I did fancy her. We were more like mates, or maybe Laura was a replacement for Jas. That *is* how it felt at times – she was almost the right age, and she liked the same crappy chick flicks and TV shows that Jas had forced me to watch. Being with Laura took my mind off Jas, and I would have moved into her flat if I could have. I was happy when I was with her. I asked her a few questions about Taz, but she ignored them. She called working at Dice the worst experience of her life. I didn't push it.

I'd stayed over, and Laura was in the shower. The flat was small – one bedroom, a living room, and a small kitchen and bathroom – but it was cool. The floors were stripped oak, light and smooth, and the bay window in the living room let in loads of light. The furniture was all designer stuff – the kind of thing you saw on home improvement shows. The walls were done in neutral tones like caramel and ivory. Everything looked new, which made me wonder whether Laura had money. She hadn't worked since we'd met, and the furniture had to come from somewhere.

Thinking that it was a strange place to put a newspaper, I pulled it out. It was copy of the *Leicester Mercury*, folded in half so that the back page showed. I unfolded it – then heard Laura open the bathroom door.

'What have you got there?' she asked as I turned to the front page and saw the main headline. I recognized it because I knew it. The edition that had carried Jennifer Barton's story about Anita Athwal and Jas. Something flipped in my chest and my mouth went dry.

'*Sat?*'

I turned to face her, held up the paper. 'What's this?' I asked, watching her face intently, looking for signs. Was I being set up? Had Laura been lying to me?

'It's a newspaper,' she said dismissively, as though I was stupid. Her hair, still damp from the shower, was slicked back on her head. She wore a black vest top and oversized jersey boxers in pale grey. Her feet were bare.

'Why have you got it?' I replied. 'Why *this* newspaper?'

Laura came over and took it out of my hands. She

stared at it and shrugged. 'It's just a newspaper,' she repeated. 'What's the big deal?'

I shook my head. 'There aren't any other newspapers on the shelf . . . Just that one . . .'

Laura gave me a funny look. 'And that means *what* exactly?'

'That newspaper . . . the date—'

'You're talking shit, Sat,' she interrupted. 'What's got *into* you?'

I looked at the paper in her hands before taking it back. I opened it at the article about Anita Athwal, the one with my picture, showing Laura. This time something in her eyes changed.

'What?' She looked away, towards the window.

'Why did you keep *this* paper?' I asked again. 'Why *this* date – is there something personal in it?'

Laura walked over to the sofa and sat down. My khaki Adidas top was lying on the floor by her feet. She picked it up, straightening it out.

'Laura?'

'What's the big deal?' she asked, only this time there was no argument in her tone. She was almost whispering, and her face had lost its colour, turning ghostly pale.

Instead of shouting, I walked over and sat by her side. I could see that something was seriously wrong. She had to know that the article was about Jas and

201

me too. Laura shuddered as I joined her. She was still holding my top.

'This article . . .' I said softly, holding the paper in front of her. 'It's about a missing woman. And it's about me too.'

Laura looked at the picture of Anita Athwal and nodded slowly. Then she let her left index finger linger on the smaller photo of me.

'I know,' she replied.

'Is that something to you?'

She looked away.

'Well, is it?'

She turned back to me and nodded. 'I know,' she repeated. 'I know who you are, Sat.'

Then she started to sob.

Much later, I sat there silently while Laura went through everything. How she'd met Taz at a bar when she was a Year Ten. How they'd started seeing each other. That he'd been charming and kind, and caring too. She told me about working at Dice, about Taz and Ricky and their businesses. She explained about the flat, the furniture, even her car – how Taz had paid for it all. Then she told me that they'd split up and Taz was going to throw her out.

'Did you know my sister?' I asked when she ran out of explanations.

'No,' she replied. 'Taz never brought her to work.'

'What about pictures? Did he show you pictures of his wife?'

Laura nodded. 'He said that she was . . .'

'*What*? That she was *what*?' I snapped.

'It doesn't matter, Sat,' said Laura.

I looked into her eyes. 'It matters to me,' I told her. 'Is this some sick joke?'

'*No!*' she screamed at me. 'That's horrible . . . Why would I *do* that?'

'Strange, though,' I continued. 'You and me suddenly hook up, straight after all my trouble with Ricky and Taz.'

'What trouble?'

'Like you don't know,' I scoffed, instantly annoyed at my tone.

Laura shook her head. 'I don't know everything they do. But I know they were pissed off about the article – I overheard them talking to Johnny.'

'Johnny?'

'The doorman that gave you grief at New Year's.'

'Who's he, then?'

'He's a psycho,' said Laura. 'They all work together – Johnny supplies the doormen and any other thugs they need.'

'Tall black guy?' I asked. 'Built like a horse with a cannonball for a head . . . ?'

Laura nodded. 'Otis Blackwood,' she replied. 'He's another nutcase. Taz said he went inside for an acid attack on his ex-wife. She was seeing a new bloke and Otis didn't like it. He scarred her for life.'

'Nice people.'

'I'm not one of them,' Laura protested. 'I never was. I was just with Taz – that's all.'

'Even after you knew he'd got married?'

Laura gave me a blank look. 'He said that it was just tradition. To keep his mum happy. That it was just for show and I was his real woman . . .'

'And that didn't bother you?' I added. 'My sister didn't matter?'

'How *could* she matter when I didn't *know* her? I was with Taz and I was stupid – believing what he told me and . . .'

Despite my anger, I knew that Laura was right. *Taz* was to blame for what happened – just Taz.

'Do you know what happened to my sister?' I asked.

This time Laura took hold of my hands. 'No,' she whispered.

'Nothing at all?'

She looked into my eyes and sighed. 'Taz set up all these fake accounts,' she told me. 'He got me to create a joke Facebook page. Said it was for a friend – to wind him up. I didn't know what he was doing. Then, when I was off my head with booze and gear, he asked me to make up text messages. I didn't think about it because I was out of it. It's only when I read the article that I remembered what happened with Ricky's wife – how she ran off and Ricky was angry for ages. Taz told me about it. I had no reason to think he was lying – not at first.'

I shot out of the sofa and went over to the window. My stomach was churning. I had proof that Taz had invented the Facebook page and all the other stuff.

'Didn't you get suspicious when he asked you to fake things?' I asked, not looking at her.

'I don't *know*,' protested Laura. 'I was drunk and coked up. My head was wrong, Sat . . . like it wasn't really *me*. The drugs aren't an excuse, but I haven't *got* anything else. I know it was wrong – that's why I left. Eventually . . .'

I turned back to her and shook my head. 'This is so wrong,' I said quietly. 'It's just all wrong . . .'

'I know,' she whispered.

'I can't stay here,' I told her. 'This isn't right . . .'

Before she could say another word, I grabbed my top and stormed out of the flat. I heard her calling me back but I ignored her.

I walked out onto Queens Road. My head felt like a road in an earthquake zone, cracked, blistered, broken. My thoughts had turned to rubble. Everything I had suspected was true – and it didn't matter.

What was I going to do with the information? If I went to the police, Taz would hurt my family. All I had was Laura's word. Yet keeping quiet would kill me. I'd never be free of the guilt and anger I felt over Jas. I felt stuck, with no idea what to do next.

TWENTY

I ignored Laura's calls for a few days. She rang constantly, leaving one message after another. Eventually I set my phone's profile to silent. It didn't stop the calls. I sat around at home, thinking about my life, desperate to get away from my family. I could no longer escape to school: I needed a job, a place to live, both of which would be tough to find. I was too young, with no qualifications and no money of my own. My family provided everything I had – none of it was really mine. I felt like I was going mad.

Amar and Mandy had moved in again, having rented out their own house. Although I enjoyed seeing Aran, who was growing fast, I felt caged in. Living at home felt like torture. My parents seemed happier because of my nephew, but underneath things weren't right. Dad was still drinking every night and Mum had stopped going out. She didn't even visit her friends' houses.

No one mentioned Jas: it was as if she'd never existed. As if she had died, and talking about her would only cause more pain. The few photographs of her were gone, replaced by hastily framed pictures of Aran. The picture of us together at Disney World was still in my room, though, sitting on my desk – a constant reminder of happier times. Even without the photographs, Jas's face stayed with me day and night. In the mornings I had peace for maybe an hour, tops, before she walked into my thoughts. I dreamed about meeting her in town or on the bus. She asked me why I wasn't trying to find her. Why I hadn't told the police about Laura and the fake messages. I tried to tell her that I was scared of the Atwals – convinced that they'd hurt our family, but she didn't listen. She sounded hurt and angry, and sent waves of guilt crashing through my heart. It was constant; it gnawed at me, eating away at my nerves.

Four days after finding out about Laura, I got a text message from Charlotte. I read it twice before calling her.

'What are you on about?' I asked.

'I want to know.' Her voice was cold.

'I haven't got another girl,' I protested.

'Don't lie, Sat. I saw you together . . .'

I sighed. She must have been talking about Laura. I felt bad that she'd seen us and realized that I should have told her myself. Not that there was anything to tell.

'Where did you see me?' I asked.

Charlotte waited a moment. 'Walking down Queens Road,' she said eventually. 'Arm in arm – with her. Did you think I wouldn't find out?'

I started to laugh, hoping to defuse things. Bad move.

'*Don't laugh at me!*' she shouted.

'I'm not, babe,' I said quickly. 'That's just Laura.'

'Laura?'

I wondered how much to tell her. 'She's just a mate. Someone I hang out with.'

Charlotte took a deep breath. 'She's the girl from Dice – I recognized her.'

'So?' I asked, getting annoyed. 'You're the one who wanted space. So what if I've got other friends?'

'Is *that* what she is?' said Charlotte, her voice thick with sarcasm. 'Only she used to work at Taz's bar – you know, the brother-in-law you don't like?'

'*And?*'

'And all of a sudden she's your best mate? You must think I'm stupid . . .'

I sighed again. 'I don't think that. I just don't see why it's any of your business. *You* walked away, remember?'

'I *didn't* walk away,' she said. 'I wanted to concentrate on my education. It's not the same thing.'

'Well,' I said, getting angry, 'while you were concentrating on that, I needed someone to talk to. And I talk to Laura.'

The line went dead.

Twenty minutes later I was sitting at Charlotte's kitchen table with a mug of tea. She sat opposite me, her face set. She was wearing a blue dress with purple flowers printed on it. Her hair was tied up, her feet bare, which only reminded me of Laura. In turn, thinking about Laura made me feel guilty, angry and sad, all at the same time.

'Explain, then,' Charlotte demanded. 'You've got five minutes.'

'Don't be like that,' I pleaded. 'I'm not your enemy.'

She turned away, her eyes moist. 'You and me,' she said softly, 'we just don't work. You're stuck with this thing and I can't help you.'

'This *thing*? Is that what Jas is, then?'

Charlotte shook her head, still looking at something else. 'I didn't mean it like that. It's just that you're throwing your life away. When we met, you were exciting and different. Now you're moody all the time. I know it's hard for you, but—'

I cut her off. 'You don't know,' I told her. 'If you really understood, you wouldn't be pissed off.'

Charlotte looked into my eyes. 'I'm sixteen, Sat,' she said. 'I want to be happy and carefree. This thing with Jas is too much for me. I'm just trying to be honest.'

'So why do you care about Laura?'

'Because I don't like being lied to. You only had to say . . .'

I groaned. 'Say what?' I replied. 'She's someone who knows about Taz. She's someone I can talk to. She listens to me and doesn't make me feel guilty when I get upset over Jas.'

A small tear rolled down Charlotte's right cheek. 'I know you think I'm a bitch,' she said, 'but I'm not. I'm just not able to do this any more. I don't want to hang around while you sort yourself out. I'm sorry.'

I put my mug on the table. 'So we're done then?' I said angrily.

Charlotte looked down at her hands. 'I dunno . . . We don't see each other anyway.'

'You're busy with exams,' I reminded her.

'Yes, and you're busy too. Only my exams will end. You can't say the same about what you're doing, can you?'

I shrugged. 'I'm going to get them,' I said defiantly. 'I don't care how long it takes.'

'And I hope you do. But I have my own life. I can't just sit around waiting for you.'

'I never asked that, did I?'

She got up from her chair and went over to the worktop, leaning against it. Her legs were long, the skin golden. I felt an urge to touch her, to hold her and kiss her, but I knew that was all gone. Charlotte was vanishing from my life – in a different way to Jas, but she was still going all the same.

'Not in so many words,' she said. 'But that's what would happen. I mean, how long would it take? You've already messed up your GCSEs.'

I stood up too, shaking my head. 'I can retake the exams,' I pointed out. 'And besides, I don't care about them. Not more than I care about my sister.'

Charlotte came and stood in front of me, her eyes glistening. 'Leave it to the police,' she said. *Please.*'

'I can't. They won't do anything until I can get some proof.'

'Yes they can,' she insisted. 'It's what they do.'

'*No!*' I shouted.

Charlotte took a step back, shocked and angry. 'Don't shout at me,' she said quietly. 'I don't care what your problems are – I'm not to blame.'

I held up my hands. 'I'm sorry. I didn't mean to shout.'

She went back to her chair and sat down. 'Maybe when this is over . . .' she murmured, more to herself.

'You want me to go?' I asked.

She nodded but said nothing.

'Really?'

When she looked up at me, the tears were falling freely. She shrugged. 'I just can't do this,' she said. 'I'm sorry . . .'

I felt a shudder in my stomach. My throat went dry. I turned and walked away, my head in bits.

'I'm sorry,' I said aloud when I reached the front door. I felt sick for pushing her away. My thoughts flashed back to that lunchtime in Sainsbury's when I'd asked her out. The way she'd tied up her hair, the light blue dress she'd been wearing. I could still smell the vanilla scent . . .

'Sat?' I heard her say.

I turned to find her standing by the kitchen door. I walked back and gave her a hug, fighting back tears.

'I want to be friends,' she whispered as I held her.

'OK,' I said softly.

We stood like that for a while. Then I kissed her and let her go.

Two minutes later I was sitting on a weathered bench in a small park. I looked across the grass towards the playground. A girl of about ten was holding her little brother's hand. He tried to pull away but she held on tight. I looked around, saw that they were alone. Despite the frustration and hurt, I smiled to myself, thinking of Jas. How she'd take me to the park or the shops, always keeping a close eye on me, protecting me. I realized that Charlotte was right. I had no time for anything else, no space inside my head or heart. How could I expect her to deal with that? *I* couldn't have done it.

My phone began to vibrate in my pocket. I pulled it out, saw that it was Laura, and ignored the call. Only that didn't stop her. She rang back continuously, seven or eight times, until finally I relented.

TWENTY-ONE

'Yeah?'

'Talk to me. *Please?*' I heard Laura pleading as I watched the kids playing.

Semi-detached houses enclosed the park on three sides, their gardens backing onto it. A slight breeze carried the smell of frying onions and garam masala.

'What's the point?' I asked her. 'Why should I bother?'

'I know you feel hurt and angry,' she told me. 'But I can help you. I *want* to help you.'

'Because you feel guilty. That's *it*, isn't it?'

'*Please*, Sat . . .'

The boy tried to walk up the slide while his sister pulled him back. Two more kids, boys, ran over to the swings, shouting excitedly. A man came past with his dog, a powerful brindle Staff. The dog sniffed at my trainers.

'What can you say or do, Laura?' I asked. 'Nothing is gonna bring her back.'

I wondered whether I meant Jas or Charlotte. My stomach folded in on itself.

'I can help,' Laura said again. 'Give me a chance.'

Something stopped me from ending the call – maybe it was losing Charlotte. Perhaps I believed that Laura really had been played by Taz – just like my sister and my parents.

'Meet me,' said Laura. 'That bar we went to on Queens Road . . . Babelas?'

'When?' I asked, realizing that I had nothing to lose. After splitting up with Charlotte, I needed the company too.

'You tell me. I'm at home.'

'One chance,' I told Laura. 'That's all you get from me.'

'I understand. Just knock at the flat when you get here and I'll come down.'

We sat upstairs, watching the early evening crowd. Babelas was tiny, just two small rooms, one on top of the other, with a single bar on the ground floor and a set of steep wooden stairs which had been painted sunshine yellow. I was drinking lemonade, trying to keep straight. Laura sat opposite me, a pint of cider in her hand. She had her hair gelled back and wore absolutely no make-up. Her eyes were red and she looked tired. She was wearing a slate-grey wool dress, with thick black tights and scuffed black biker boots.

'I can get them,' Laura said unexpectedly.

I was busy watching a couple of middle-aged women gossiping about something. They were talking in whispers and giggling into glasses of white wine.

'Get who?' I asked, taking a sip of lemonade.

'Taz and Ricky,' she said softly, as if they might be standing behind her.

She had my attention now.

'How?' I turned my eyes towards her.

Laura leaned across the table. 'When Ricky's wife went missing, Taz, Ricky and Johnny Owens were on holiday . . . I think Otis went too.'

'So?' I asked, wondering where she was going.

'They told everyone that they were in Thailand,' she replied. 'But I know Johnny was in India. I know it for a *fact* . . .'

I thought back to the article Jennifer had written. There'd been some details about the case, but I couldn't remember them. At the time my focus had been on Jas and not Anita. Anita's brother had also mentioned things, but they were just a blur. So much had happened since then.

'Let's go,' I said.

'Where?' asked Laura.

'The flat – I need to look at the article again. I've also got Anita's brother's number in my phone . . .'

Some of Dhaminder's words had started coming back to me.

'But—'

'He told me that Ricky didn't go to India with Anita,' I continued. 'It was just Anita and Ricky's mum that went. And she went missing *in* India . . .'

In minutes we were sitting on Laura's sofa, checking Anita's story. On a family trip to India she had run off with a boyfriend. She'd prearranged it and the police had seen emails and text messages, supplied by the Athwals, which confirmed things. After running away with this mystery boyfriend, she had vanished. No one had seen her since. The parallels to Jas's story were astonishing.

'Can you remember when they went on holiday?' I asked Laura.

'Yeah. It was just before Anita went missing. I remember Taz saying that she'd asked for a divorce – wanted to take half of Ricky's money. Then she ran off while Ricky and Taz were on holiday.'

'What else?'

Laura shifted position so that she faced me. I could smell her perfume, warm and musky, and thought of Charlotte again.

'It was weird,' she went on, 'because normally when the brothers go away, Johnny looks after things. Only this time he went too. When he came back, he bragged about how many Thai girlfriends he'd had.' She shook her head, disgusted at the thought.

'And you're sure it was India?'

'Completely, Sat,' she replied. 'He was in a photo – standing in front of a temple. He told everyone it was

Thailand but it wasn't. I've never been to the Punjab, but I know what the Golden Temple looks like.'

'The Golden Temple – the one in Amritsar?' I asked.

Laura nodded. 'I remember looking it up – just to be sure,' she said. 'And if that photo is still on his phone or computer – it's evidence.'

'He could just say he went at some other time,' I pointed out.

Laura held up a hand. 'Digital cameras and phones put a timecode on photographs, don't they?' she half asked, half insisted.

I thought about it for a second. 'I have no idea. We could check.'

Laura pulled out her iPhone and tapped its screen. After a few moments she showed me a picture of a cute blonde toddler with curly hair and big rosy cheeks. The kid was grinning.

'My niece,' she explained. 'I took the photo with my old phone, just before last Christmas. Then, when I got this, I transferred the file across.'

She'd lost me, but I didn't admit to it. She tapped the phone a few more times.

'Here,' she said, showing me the screen once more. 'If you go into "details" it tells you when the file was first made. Look at the date.'

'It's from December twenty-third last year,' I said.

'Exactly,' she replied, looking excited. 'The info is

all there, even though I transferred the picture from another phone. If we can get that photo from Johnny's phone, he's finished.'

I shook my head. 'So . . . what – we just *ask* him for it?'

'We'll work something out . . . I'm sure I saw him downloading something onto Taz's PC at Dice.'

'But how do we check the computer?'

'Simple,' replied Laura. 'I need to pick up some things. As long as I go when Taz isn't around, I can take a look . . .'

'What if someone sees you?'

She shrugged. 'What's the big deal?' she asked. 'I'm just deleting my own files before I leave.'

I nodded, although I wasn't convinced.

'*Shit!*' she said suddenly, making me jump.

'What?'

'A lot of those fake messages and stuff were on Taz's hard drive . . .'

I could feel my eyes widening.

'And every file has details about dates and stuff . . .'

A sudden burst of reality dampened my excitement. 'He's probably deleted all those,' I said, but Laura shook her head.

'He hasn't got a clue about computers,' she told me. 'I did everything . . . All he does is download porn or use the idiot-proof stock system.'

'What about a password?' I asked, trying to cover all the bases.

'He rarely uses them. The few he does use are written in his diary.'

'So what now?' I didn't want to get too excited, but it was difficult not to. Suddenly, after feeling so helpless, I actually felt like we could get the Atwals. Ram the arrogance and lies down their throats.

Laura went into the kitchen and came back with a bottle of Jack Daniel's and two glasses. 'There's no cola,' she said, setting the glasses down on the table and pouring two big shots.

I looked at the amber liquid in the glasses and shrugged.

'Tomorrow's Friday,' she said, picking up her glass and turning it round in her hand. 'Taz starts late on Fridays.'

'What about Ricky?' I asked, taking up my own glass. The fumes were strong and I could almost taste the alcohol even before I put it to my lips.

'He hates me,' said Laura. 'He'll be relieved that I'm leaving – trust me.'

I nodded.

'But just to make sure . . .'

I watched as she picked up her phone and made a call. She spoke to someone called Cerys for a few minutes and then rang off.

'Sorted,' she told me. 'I'm going in at eleven a.m.'

I took a swig of whisky, wondering if I should mention breaking up with Charlotte. In the end I decided not to. It wouldn't have changed anything.

'You didn't tell me her name,' I said instead.

Laura gave me a funny look. 'Who?'

'Your niece,' I replied, making her grin.

'Anoushka . . .' she said. 'Now, you drinking or what, schoolboy?'

TWENTY-TWO

After driving past Dice four times, Laura parked down a side street. Her Mini Cooper, bright red with a white roof, felt cramped, mostly because I was restless.

'I won't be long,' she told me. 'If I get into trouble, I'll call you.'

'And then what?' I asked, stretching out my legs.

'Er . . . *help* me?'

I looked into her honey-coloured eyes. 'Are you sure about this?' I was worried about what might happen. The idea had seemed brilliant the previous evening, but the grey, overcast morning had dulled its shine.

'I'll be fine,' said Laura, trying to reassure me. 'Even if Ricky turns up, he'll just swear a bit and start getting drunk. That's all he does.'

'OK,' I said with a nod. 'Be careful though, yeah?'

'I will.' She tossed me the keys and walked off up the street.

I wondered whether she would find anything, realizing that it was our last chance. Unless Laura got proof of some sort, the Atwals were going to get away with it. Only I couldn't help thinking that we were chasing shadows. Surely the police would have looked for evidence. While I was waiting, I decided to call

Dhaminder. He answered on the fourth ring.

'It's Sat Kooner,' I told him.

'I know,' he replied, 'your name came up. You OK?'

'Yeah . . . I was just wondering something. Can you talk?'

I heard him tell someone that he was taking a break. After a few moments of rustling and doors opening, I heard a siren blaring.

'Sorry,' he said finally, 'I'm at work.'

'Is that a problem?' I asked. 'I can call back later.'

'No, no,' he assured me. 'What can I do for you?'

I got my thoughts in order. I didn't want to raise his hopes, but at the same time I needed to check some details. It was too soon to tell him what we were doing. What we were *trying* to do.

'Did the police investigate the Atwals?' I asked, hoping not to sound too direct. It didn't work.

'Why?' His voice had suddenly perked up.

'Nothing really,' I lied. 'I was just thinking that Ricky or his brother might have left some evidence. Something that might help . . .'

'The police spoke to them a few times,' he replied. 'But they were never arrested. That tells me there was nothing to find. It was all rumours, and that wasn't enough. No hard evidence, they said.'

'But how hard did they look?'

Dhaminder paused for a moment. 'Not much, until I

kicked off. Anita ran away with some bloke, according to Ricky. Because she was an adult, the police weren't overly worried. They said that adults go off all the time.'

'Yeah, they said the same about Jas,' I told him.

'They sent some domestic officers round,' he continued. 'I guess they spoke with Ricky too.'

I told him how similar my experience had been. 'Surely, after a couple of years, they can see that something is wrong.'

'That's what I think,' he said. 'But there's no evidence – other than some emails and stuff Anita supposedly sent. The first investigation was too quick. It was only when I got our MP involved that things changed.'

I sighed. 'And like you said – still nothing.'

'Nah,' he said softly. 'There's still a reward for information posted across the Punjab, but since that last time I told you about, no one has come forward.'

'You reckon the Atwals bribed people over there, in India?' I asked, fiddling with the volume button on the CD player.

'I *know* they did,' replied Dhaminder. 'I spoke to the police over there. They just went along with what Ricky said. They told me to protect my family from the shame.'

'*Really?*'

'Yeah. They were the wrong side of useless. We had witnesses too, but they went quiet all of a sudden. When

225

the British police arrived, they hit a wall of silence. That's what the lead detective called it.'

'OK,' I replied.

'Why the questions, Sat?' he asked. 'Has something happened?'

'No.' I felt bad for holding out on him. 'If anything does, I'll let you know. Trust me . . .'

'Right. I'd better get back to work, then.'

'Thanks,' I said.

''S OK,' he replied before ending the call.

I put my phone down on the driver's seat and looked out of the dirty windscreen. Maybe, just maybe, Laura was right, I thought. Perhaps she'd find something on Taz's PC that would help us. She seemed sure that Johnny Owens had visited India. Why would he lie about it? Something was wrong with that – *had* to be. The link was Anita and India, and if we could prove that Johnny Owens had been present when she disappeared, we were in business.

As I was thinking this, Ricky's Jaguar went by. I threw myself across the driver's seat, praying that he hadn't seen me. The Jaguar didn't slow down or stop. At the end of the street the brake lights lit up and it turned onto the main road. I panicked and grabbed my phone.

'Just relax,' Laura told Sat. 'He's not going to do anything.'

She ended his call and returned to her task. Sitting at Taz's desk, she searched through the hundreds of files, trying to find something that stuck out. There were numerous folders entitled 'Taz-Private', each with a different number attached. Yet when Laura opened them, all she found was porn – at least two gigabytes worth. She shuddered at the memory of sharing a bed with Taz, and went on searching.

The first break came just as Ricky walked into the office.

'Why are you here?' he demanded, eyeing her with suspicion.

'Getting my stuff,' she replied. 'Why?'

'Because you don't belong here – you never have.'

'Taz knows I'm here,' said Laura, taking a chance. 'I told him I had to tie up some stuff, and he was fine with it.'

Ricky snorted. 'Probably just glad to see the back of you.'

Laura looked at him and felt revulsion. 'Not as glad as I am,' she retorted. 'Now he can shag as many slappers as he likes . . .'

'That's how he met you, innit?'

Laura swore at Ricky and went back to the screen.

'Just get what you need and piss off,' he said.

'I was doing that — until you bought your cheap-smelling arse in here,' she replied.

'What you at the computer for anyway?'

Laura felt her heart sink. She needed a story — and fast. 'Stock system,' she said quickly. 'I set it up, and if I don't sort it, you lot are stuffed.'

'Stock?' Ricky looked confused.

'Yeah — that stuff that you think comes for free.'

'My bar, my stock,' he replied.

'There's a load of admin too,' Laura continued. 'Letters and other stuff that has to get wiped . . .'

Ricky gave her another suspicious look. 'What stuff?' he asked, walking towards her.

Laura made an effort not to flinch. 'OK,' she said. 'You know that this bar fiddles its tax and VAT returns, don't you?'

'So?' He shrugged.

'So . . . who do you think helps with that?' Laura said slowly. 'You and your cokehead mates or me?'

Ricky watched Laura click on a folder called 'HiddenSTUFF4'.

'If you want to hide things,' she explained, 'you don't put them in folders with "Hidden" in the title. That's just stupid . . .'

'So what are you doing, then?' asked Ricky, looking even more confused.

'I'm transferring all the info onto memory sticks and wiping it from the hard drive,' she replied. 'That way Taz can hide them somewhere else. If anything happens, there's no evidence on the computers.'

'Why you helping us?' asked Ricky.

'Because I'm part of it. You get done, I get done . . .'

Laura prayed that Ricky would fall for it, counted on his lack of brains. In reality Taz was finance director for all the companies they owned. There was not a single piece of paper with Laura's name on it. The only people liable for prosecution were the listed owners and directors – Taz, Johnny and Ricky himself.

'Just get it done,' he said eventually. 'I'm grabbing some breakfast. You best be gone when I get back.'

I will be, thought Laura. *I'll be gone with copies of all of your dodgy tax and VAT receipts, and hopefully much, much more.*

'Bye . . .' she replied, opening yet another folder.

Ricky left, muttering something under his breath. When he'd gone, Laura opened 'SamsungToccoTXTS'. Inside she found a sub-folder – 'PRIVATE7'. She double-clicked the icon and opened a list of text messages, dated and in neat rows. She opened the first, saw that she'd composed it, and cursed herself. A pang of guilt stabbed at her. She connected two 8GB memory sticks to USB ports, one for Taz and one for her. The first stick was her cover story, holding the sensitive information she'd shown to Ricky. The second was for her and Sat. It was the evidence they needed.

Over the next hour Laura found most of what she was after. Taz had left everything in plain sight, including details of passwords for the fake Hotmail, Facebook, Yahoo and Gmail accounts that he'd set up for Jas. Yet it was all insignificant compared to a password-protected folder titled 'HOLIDAY'. Knowing that Taz was obsessed with James Bond films and used them as passwords, Laura worked chronologically, first 007 film to last. At 'Moonraker' the file opened.

'Shit . . .' she whispered. Taz was even more stupid than she'd realized. She cursed herself again for her choice of man.

There were forty-two photographs in the folder.

Taz, Ricky, Johnny Owens and Otis Blackwood were in most of them – all taken in India. Laura checked the properties of the first photo. The dates matched the time when Anita Athwal went missing. They clearly showed that the Atwal brothers had been in the Punjab at the same time. Laura whooped with delight and copied the folder quickly.

'You OK?' she heard Cerys say from the office door.

Laura looked up at her and smiled. 'Ecstatic,' she replied. 'I've wasted too much of my life in this shithole.'

Cerys nodded. 'I'm leaving too. That Ricky keeps trying it on. I'll end up stabbin' him in the head if I stay.'

'Good girl!'

Cerys asked Laura if she wanted a drink.

'Oh, why not? Big JD and Coke – I'll be out in a minute.'

Once Cerys was gone, Laura looked over at the safe. The keys were stuck in the door – one more sign of Taz and Ricky's arrogance. She turned the keys and pulled open the heavy iron door. Realizing that she had very little time, she rifled through the contents. She ignored the bundles of cash, tempting as they were, and concentrated on the documents. Nothing stood out as important until she found a passport. She took it out, opened it and let out a little scream. Her heart was working overtime.

The passport went into her bag, and before she closed the safe, some of the cash followed. Laura locked up, double-checked that she had everything, and went over to Taz's PC. She opened a new Word file and chose a huge red font before tapping at the keys.

'Have that, you bastard . . .' she said, walking out of the office for the last time. Behind her on the monitor, in giant letters, were the words: 'GOODBYE NEEDLE DICK.'

TWENTY-THREE

My heart wouldn't stop hammering.

'They *can't* be that stupid!' I repeated for the third time.

Laura frowned. She'd changed into a grey vest and lilac pyjama bottoms. Her feet were bare again.

'Maybe they aren't,' she said. We were back at her flat, going through all the information she'd taken from Taz. 'Maybe they're so arrogant, they think they're untouchable.'

'Not any more.' I got out my mobile phone.

'What are you doing?' she asked.

'Calling the police. Detective Inspector Elliot gave me her number.'

Laura put her hand on mine. 'Wait,' she said.

I stared at her. 'What for?'

She shrugged. 'We need to think it through. This might not be enough.'

I gave her an incredulous look. 'How can it not be *enough*? Everything we need is right there. We've got them.'

'Yeah, but I stole the information,' she pointed out. 'Not to mention the cash and the passport.'

I picked up Anita Athwal's passport and looked at it. 'This,' I said, 'is the final nail in the coffin. There's no way Anita could have gone to India without it. Which means that if the Atwals had it, they *must* have been in India when Anita was there. How did they get it otherwise?'

Laura shook her head. 'The mum could have brought it back with her?'

I laughed. 'Bollocks!' I replied. 'For a start, would *you* do a runner and leave your passport behind?'

She shook her head again.

'Exactly – nor would I. There's the photos too. Why would they lie about being in India?'

'I'm just trying to cover every possibility,' she told me.

'Stuff them. Let the police deal with it.'

Laura told me to hang on. 'I *stole* that money,' she said.

'So? Like the police are going to care! We have evidence that they lied about Anita. We have proof that they fiddle their taxes too. They're stuffed.'

'But how does that help you find Jas?'

I wanted an instant reply but it wasn't there. I knew what Laura was getting at.

'There's nothing concrete,' she continued.

'Yes there is. The fake accounts for Hotmail and Facebook.'

'OK,' she agreed. 'But there's no passport – nothing that tells us where Jas went.'

Reality smashed its way into my head, causing my stomach to turn somersaults. I felt myself grow cold – cold and certain.

'She'd dead, isn't she,' I said rather than asked.

'We don't know that,' Laura replied softly.

'We do. They lied about Anita and we know they were in India – we've got the proof. They did something to Anita. And if they did something to her, they definitely hurt Jas too.'

Laura started to reply but stopped short. I could feel my eyes filling with tears.

'Oh shit . . .' I whispered.

'Sat . . .'

'I didn't think about that,' I said. 'What finding all this stuff would mean for Jas.'

Laura put her arm around my shoulder. 'We know they hid the truth,' she replied, trying to console me. 'But we don't know exactly what happened, not yet.'

'Yes we do,' I insisted. 'We *do*.'

'Sat, come on. Until we know for sure . . .'

I didn't hear the rest of her words. My mouth started to twitch and my body convulsed. Rib-shaking sobs erupted from my belly.

Laura stopped talking and held onto me.

We ended up in Laura's bed – just lying there. She fell asleep quickly, even though it was mid-afternoon.

I watched her chest rising and falling as I thought through the hopes and fears that swam around inside my head. I replayed everything I'd done since Jas disappeared; all the times when I had been angry or scared – distraught one minute and full of purpose the next. Now, with Laura's evidence in my hands, I was close to getting what I wanted. So close to the truth that I could feel it, smell it, taste it. Only it tasted of despair, it smelled of failure and felt as if thousands of hammers were beating my hopes into dust. Jas was dead – I knew it. She would never come back, never smile again, never be my sister. She'd be a memory, a silent presence, some half-remembered dream.

Laura woke up a little while later and turned to me. 'I like you,' she said, putting her hand on my face.

'I like you too,' I told her.

She shook her head. 'Not just like *that*,' she said. 'You're a good person, Sat.'

'Really?'

'Really. You care about things and you're sensitive. I like that.'

I put my arm round her, edging closer. 'You don't know me, really,' I said.

Laura smiled. I could smell her perfume; feel the heat of her body.

'I know enough,' she replied. 'You've given up your life to find out about Jas. That's special – at least, *I* think it is.'

'My girlfriend left me,' I said suddenly.

'I guessed as much,' said Laura. 'You don't really talk about her.'

I shrugged, taking a deep breath. 'Nothing to say . . . It had been coming.'

'Are we gonna call the police?' Laura moved closer still, changing the subject.

'Because Charlotte left me?' I joked.

She smiled and called me a dickhead.

'Yeah,' I told her. 'I'll call DI Elliot in a minute. Aren't you worried that Taz will miss the money, though?'

She shook her head. 'He won't touch it yet. The weekend tills are cashed up by Cerys and left in the safe. He does a full count on Mondays, which is stupid. But it suits us.'

'You're going to have to leave this place.'

'I know. And I don't care. To be honest, I feel sick just being here, even now. I feel like a prostitute.'

'I don't think badly of you,' I said. 'I think you just met the wrong bloke, that's all.'

Laura sighed. 'I knew what he did, though – not with Jas or Anita, but the other stuff. The drugs and the gangster bullshit. I'm still living in his flat, still driving his car . . . What does that say about me?'

'I understand that,' I said, 'but I'm not judging you because of it.'

'I know.' She smiled. 'That's why I like you.'

237

'I like you too.'

'Er . . . we've been here already,' said Laura, grinning slyly.

'Oh yeah.'

Laura placed her hand on my chest. The hairs on the back of my neck stood up.

'So what do we do now?' she said, her lips almost touching mine.

'You tell me,' I said, trying to stay cool.

'How about this?' she whispered, before kissing me.

Otis Blackwood opened the brown paper envelope and counted the cash. The manager of the bar watched him.

"'S all there, Otis,' he said.

'Best be . . .'

Once he was satisfied, Otis stuffed the cash back into the envelope, the envelope into the pocket of his leather coat. He stood up and stretched his weary body. His head pounded and he was hungry.

'You want a drink?' asked the bar manager.

Otis shook his oversized head and grinned. 'If I wanted one, I would have taken one.'

The manager, a pale, thin Geordie with pockmarked, sallow skin and tired eyes, laughed nervously, watching Otis's every movement.

'Same time next week,' Otis told him.

'No problem,' replied the man.

Otis brushed imaginary dust from his leather coat and walked out of the bar. His diamond-black VW Touareg sat right outside, half hanging off the pavement. He got in and started the engine. The sound of dancehall reggae filled the SUV. Reaching across, Otis opened the glove compartment and shoved the envelope of cash in with the rest.

One more visit and he could turn his attention to food. Otis was a night man. He liked to breakfast sometime after three in the afternoon. Saturdays were the worst day of his week. The only day when he had to rise like every other fool – early. Still, a man had to earn a crust, make a few dollars. It couldn't be helped. There were things that needed to be paid for; a few kids to support. Kids he wasn't allowed to see but still got the bill for.

He turned into the traffic, cutting in front of a taxi, and set a course for his next destination. He took side streets out of the city centre and turned left onto Regent Road, heading up towards Victoria Park. Just before De Montfort Hall, he cut right and sped down University Road, running a red light. At the top he took another left and drove towards Clarendon Park, passing a hand carwash, a few shops and rows of terraced houses. He turned left again into Greenhill Road and continued for three hundred metres until he found a parking spot. He jumped out, found the right house and slammed a meaty fist against the door.

He was in and out in five minutes, the profits pocketed, new stash safely delivered. Satisfied with his day's work, he wondered where to get a drink. He settled on a bar with a reputation for good tapas. The drive took less than five minutes. He left the SUV and took a pack of cigarettes out of his pocket. As he lit one, he saw someone he recognized. A skinny Asian lad . . .

Otis recognized the boy and the house he'd just emerged from. On the first floor was a flat owned by Taz Atwal. Laura, Taz's on/off girl, lived there. The lad was Sat Kooner, the kid Ricky had wanted to scare. Otis took precisely five seconds to work out that something wasn't right. He pulled out his phone as he watched the boy walk away.

'Yeah, John, you need to hear this,' he said.

'I'm down the gym . . . What's up?' Johnny Owens gasped.

'That kid – the one Ricky got trouble with?'

'Yeah . . . ?'

'Jus' seen him leavin' Laura's yard – the one Taz owns on Queens Road.'

'I'll call you back in five,' said Johnny. 'Don't move.'

Johnny Owens, covered in a thick layer of sweat, called Ricky Atwal.

'Where are you?' he asked.

Ricky told him that he was at the Dance Factory, going through some insurance paperwork with Taz.

'Is Taz done with that bitch?' asked Johnny.

'Which one?' Ricky joked. 'He's had a few.'

'Laura.'

'Where you at?' asked Ricky. 'You sound out of breath.'

'Gym,' Johnny told him. 'Answer the question.'

'Why – you want her?'

Johnny swore under his breath. 'Just answer the question, Ricky!'

A young woman sitting at the pectoral fly looked up. Johnny glared at her until she stopped eyeing him.

'Nah,' said Ricky. 'She grabbed all her stuff yesterday.'

'She still at the flat?'

'Yeah – until Monday,' Ricky told him. 'Why – Janis kicked you out again?'

'Shut up and listen. Does she know that little Asian lad – the one we talked to the other day?'

'What lad?'

'That Kooner kid.'

Johnny heard Ricky take a deep breath. 'Laura and Sat?'

'Yeah. Otis is on a stash run. He's just seen the kid coming out of Laura's flat.'

Ricky started swearing as Johnny fought to hold onto his patience.

'Put Taz on,' he demanded.

Johnny heard Ricky call his brother over.

'What's up?' asked Taz when he came to the phone.

Johnny explained what Otis had seen and asked what was going on.

'I don't know.' Taz's voice was grim. 'But something ain't right. Tell Otis to follow the kid. Now!'

Johnny ended the call and speed-dialled Otis. 'It's me,' he said into the handset. 'Follow him.'

'You want me to hold him?'

'No – follow him until I get back to you.'

'What if I lose him?'

'Don't . . .'

In the Dance Factory Taz turned to his brother. 'What do you mean?' he asked.

'She said that you knew,' explained Ricky. 'She was sorting through the files on the computer, deleting shit.'

'Deleting what? She wasn't supposed to touch the computer.'

Ricky frowned. 'She copied it all to a memory stick – all the stuff about tax and VAT. The stuff she helped you with.'

Taz shook his head. 'I stopped telling her that stuff ages ago . . .' he told his brother.

'The lying little bitch!'

'What else did she take?'

'I dunno,' admitted Ricky. 'I went to get breakfast.'

'You left her on her own? In the office – with all that stuff on my computer . . . ?'

Ricky shrugged.

'She's working with Sat,' said Taz.

'No way. Why would she do that?'

Taz sighed. 'She's in the office, copying files onto a memory stick, and the next thing, Otis sees Sat Kooner coming out of the flat? Think, Ricky, *think!*'

'What?'

'She's playin' us, bro. Taking the evidence about the VAT and— FUCK!'

Ricky jumped.

'Everything is on that computer,' continued Taz.

'So what?'

'You don't get it, bro,' said Taz. 'You know them photos from India?'

Ricky's eyes grew wider. 'What about them?'

'They was on there. And all them other bits – the emails and texts we shown the Kooners . . .'

'Nah – she wouldn't do that . . .' Ricky said.

'Where's the safe keys?' asked Taz.

'In the safe — in there.' Ricky nodded towards the Dance Factory office.

'Not *them*, you dickhead — the ones for Dice!'

Ricky's face fell. 'In the office,' he said quietly. 'They were there when Laura . . .'

Taz dialled Johnny's number as Ricky smashed his fist into the nearest wall.

Laura got Sat's answerphone for the fifth time. Annoyed, she went over to the window and looked down into the street. A light drizzle had begun to fall and the sky was dark. She could see Bar Dos, across the road to the left, and thought about going for a drink. To the right, she watched a gang of students walk past Queen's Tandoori before stopping at the kebab shop, looking at the menu. A police car went by, slowing when it reached Howard Road, by Yan's Hair Salon, then turning left. She heard someone shouting but couldn't see who. Then she saw it. A familiar car mounted the kerb outside Bargain Booze. A big man with powerful shoulders and thighs wider than barrels got out. He looked up at her and waved.

Laura quickly moved away from the window. Only she knew it was no good. Johnny had seen her. She ran to the front door and shot the two bolts home. Frantic, she found her rucksack and packed the Sony Vaio onto which she'd copied the evidence from the memory stick. She fetched the passport and the cash, and hid them behind the laptop before rushing into the bedroom. She grabbed some clothes, stuffing them into the bag too.

Back in the living room, she pulled novels off the shelves, no longer caring whether the pages creased or tore. She needed what was behind them: the money she had managed to skim from the bar – nearly three thousand pounds; losses that she had managed to hide by pilfering the cash slowly. This too went into the bag. Finally she found her perfume – Viktor & Rolf, a present from her brother. She was ready.

Edging towards the window, she peered out. Johnny was leaning against the silver hood of his Mercedes CLK, waiting patiently in the drizzle. Laura flinched as he looked up, but his focus was on something else. He turned his head to the left. Laura followed his gaze and saw them – Ricky and Taz, getting out of the Jaguar. She felt her legs grow weak. Taking deep breaths, she pulled out her phone. Sat failed to answer again, and Laura realized that something was wrong. They had to know. Maybe they'd already found him.

'Shit . . .' she said, realizing that she was on her own.

* * *

Taz told Ricky to calm down.

'Forget it,' his brother replied. 'Let's get the bitch now!'

'Keep your voice down,' Taz hissed. 'Witnesses . . .'

'Let's get into my car,' suggested Johnny. 'Looks better than standing in the rain.'

Taz nodded and followed Johnny to the CLK. Ricky waited a moment before joining them. Johnny turned the engine on and fiddled with the heating.

'She could do a runner,' Ricky insisted.

'Where to?' Johnny was looking in his rear-view mirror. 'There's only one way out of that rat hole.'

'Yeah,' agreed Taz. 'And we're parked right outside the exit. She ain't goin' nowhere, bro. Least, not by choice, you get me?'

Johnny looked at him and smiled. 'Silly little cow,' he said. 'I'm going to *enjoy* this . . .'

TWENTY-FOUR

On the way home I realized my phone was dead. Once I got back, I tried to find my charger, but it was gone. Mandy was at the kitchen table, holding Aran and talking to my mum. I asked her if she'd seen it.

'The Nokia one?' she replied, her attention focused on my nephew, who was starting to cry.

'Yeah.'

'Amar took it with him to the newsagent's,' she told me. 'I think there's another one in the living room.'

I shook my head. 'It's for your BlackBerry.'

'Don't Asda sell them?'

The rain was getting heavier, driving against the kitchen window. I shook my head. 'I'm not going out in that.'

'If I get a minute later on, I'll drive you.'

'Thanks,' I said, silently cursing my brother.

DI Elliot's card was in my pocket, burning a hole. I had enough evidence to get Taz now. Maybe I wouldn't get him for Jas, but I *would* get him. I went into the living room, found the house phone and dialled her number. After six rings her answerphone kicked in. I ignored it and rang off. Underneath her mobile number was the direct line at the station. I called that instead, and someone answered straight away.

'DI Elliot's phone,' the man said.

'Er . . . I was trying to reach Miss Elliot,' I said uncertainly.

'Yes, sir. The DI is away from her desk. Can I take a message?'

I said I'd try her mobile again.

'She's on leave this weekend,' the man informed me. 'I can have her call you back on Monday morning.'

I considered telling him what was going on, but something stopped me. I trusted Elliot and wanted to talk to her. I wanted to tell her about Ricky's threats, ask her about protection for my family.

'It's not urgent,' I lied. 'I'll call back on Monday.'

I went to my room and booted up the computer. As usual, it took ages and I felt myself growing impatient. I wondered what Laura was doing. Whether she was thinking about what we'd found out. Or maybe about what we'd done with each other. Laura was in a bad place inside her head. Taz had lied to her for a long time. Not as much as he'd lied to my family, but enough. The guilt had to be massive – now that she knew about him. I wondered how much it would bother her. Was she like me – unable to get away from her thoughts? Maybe she was one of those people who could just get on with things. I looked at the memory stick she'd given me.

No matter what, she had made up for her mistakes.

Once the computer was ready, I logged on to Facebook. There were no messages on Jas's page, and none on mine either. I switched to the other sites I'd created – still nothing. I checked out various missing persons websites too, just killing time. I missed dinner but I wasn't hungry anyway, and around midnight I got myself a drink of water. The house was silent and cold. I went into the living room, hoping that Amar had replaced my charger, but no such luck. I cussed him again and went back to my bedroom.

I slept badly, my dreams full of Jas and the Atwals. I dreamed I was talking to DI Elliot, sitting in a courtroom, watching Taz on trial. I had never been into a courtroom. The one in my dream came from an episode of *Law and Order* I'd seen. Then I was sitting in Laura's flat, waiting for her. The bathroom door opened and I looked up, smiling. Smiling back at me, like a giant reptile with dead eyes, was Johnny Owens. I sat up in bed, sweating and shaking.

It was early Sunday afternoon before I woke up. I rubbed my eyes and swore. I needed to call Laura, tell her that DI Elliot wasn't around until Monday. Only I didn't know Laura's number – it was on my dead Nokia. I jumped out of bed and into the shower. Ten minutes later I was dressed and in the kitchen, eating a piece of toast with Marmite. My mum fussed over Aran as Mandy compiled a shopping list.

'Did Amar bring my charger back?' I asked, wondering if it was in their bedroom.

'I dunno,' she said. 'You want me to get you one?'

I nodded. 'I've got some cash upstairs,' I told her.

'Don't be silly.' She smiled at me. 'I'm sure I can stretch to a phone charger, Sat. We're family.'

The last two words cut through me. Ricky's face appeared in my mind, telling me the same thing, before threatening to kill us. I looked at Aran, who was beaming at my mum.

'You OK?' I heard Mandy ask.

'Yeah,' I replied. 'Leave the charger – I'll get one. I want to go for a walk anyway.'

Mum looked up at me. 'Remember we have a wedding party tonight,' she told me in Punjabi.

I shrugged. 'Not going,' I said.

'I'm telling you.' She was getting annoyed.

'No,' I said without raising my voice. 'I'm going out with my mates.'

'Is that where you stayed on Friday night?' she asked. 'Wandering in like a dog on Saturday . . . Have you no shame?'

She carried on, doing my head in. Aran looked up at me and chuckled. I took him, held him to my shoulder, sniffed at his head. The warm baby scent calmed

252

me down. When my mum was done giving me grief, I walked Aran around the kitchen, talking shit, like people do with babies. He didn't seem to mind. He just carried on making gurgling sounds, his eyes wide and alert.

'You'll make a good dad,' said Mandy.

I shook my head. 'Not for a long time yet,' I told her, warding off any talk of marriage.

Mandy had a cousin called Preet who was around my age. She mentioned her regularly and wound me up. That's how things were done in my family. One minute they'd be joking about some girl, the next you'd be sitting in a *gurdwara*, turban on your head, getting married. Forget that.

'I have to go out,' I said. 'Here, take Aran.'

'Put him in the rocker,' she told me. 'Make sure the buckles are done up.'

'I'm not stupid,' I replied, doing as she asked.

Aran looked like he might cry, so I tried to soothe him. Mum came back into the kitchen and took over.

'See you later,' I said to them all.

'The party's in Birmingham,' Mandy said. 'We're leaving at six, if you change your mind.'

I nodded.

The walk to Asda took fifteen minutes but I wasted some time calling in on Dash. His drive was empty and no one answered. I turned, walking back the way I'd come. The clouds were dark grey, like the slate on roofs, and I knew the rain would come again. I hurried along, taking a short cut through an alley. I was oblivious to the world around me, my mind taken up with the usual thoughts. I passed an old man walking a tiny white dog, a group of three teenage girls, all dressed up after a trip into town, and a woman pushing a pram that had three wheels.

The short cut took me onto the main A6, towards Asda. I walked quickly, anxious to get there before I was soaked. A single fat droplet landed on my shoulder, like an advance scout preparing for an invasion. I looked up and groaned. I was going to get drenched. As a second and third raindrop hit me, I saw a black VW Touareg R50 moving slowly towards me. The paintwork gleamed, despite the gloom, the headlights and grille giving me an evil smile. I froze as it pulled in to the kerb and Otis Blackwood got out.

'Get in,' he said, his face set in a grimace, his eyes like daggers.

Before I could move, before I even considered running, Otis was in my face, holding me by the shoulder, his hand a tightening vice.

TWENTY-FIVE

Otis Blackwood drove slowly. I was in the back, Johnny Owens sitting beside me holding a black gun. Neither man spoke, other than to warn me.

'One move . . .' was all Johnny said. I understood. I was too scared to do anything anyway. My limbs felt frozen.

We hit the outer ring road, heading north-east around the city. I tried to breathe normally as we passed a new sixth-form college, a large Tesco and a Porsche garage. I was so scared, my legs twitched. My chest felt like it would cave in. Either that or explode. I thought about my family, getting ready to go to Birmingham, and wondered if I would ever see them again. Better me, I told myself. Better me than my dad or my brother. *I* was the one who'd pushed Taz, wound him up. It was all my doing.

We turned left at a roundabout, into an industrial estate. The rain was thundering down, creating deep puddles for the Touareg to splash through. There were no people about, no witnesses. Anyone with a brain was inside, out of the storm. I had just walked into one. Otis drove past row after row of units until he spotted a turning – just a gravel track really – to the right. He took it and I heard stones twanging off the car's fat bumpers. About five hundred yards later he stopped, turning to face Johnny.

'You want me to wait?' he asked. He looked like a horse leaning over a stable door. I'd never seen such a big jaw.

'Nah,' Johnny replied. 'You're coming in.'

He told me to follow him. 'Don't try anything,' he warned. 'You can't get away.'

I nodded and stepped out into the downpour. An old two-storey industrial unit stood before us. It had three loading bays at the front. To the right of the bays was a small door. Johnny headed towards it, cussing the rain. He struck it three times, his fists like giant hams. Someone drew a bolt and the door fell open with a metallic groan.

'In,' he ordered.

We entered a giant open space. Several office cubicles were arranged around the perimeter, with two metal staircases in each of the far corners. Only the stairs didn't lead anywhere. There were signs of building work too: ladders, paint, bare electrics, and pallets of concrete blocks. Ricky was waiting for me.

'You don't listen, do you?' he said, shaking his head.

Nothing I said would matter, so I stayed silent. There was no getting out of it now. I was in serious trouble. I looked around, wondering where Taz was.

'Take him over there,' Ricky told Johnny. He pointed towards one of the offices.

Johnny gave me a shove. 'Move!'

The office was dark and stank of mould. Old shelves lined the walls, rotting away. My trainers stuck to the floor as Johnny pushed me inside. I heard a rodent squeaking somewhere.

'We were gonna turn this into a club,' I heard Ricky say.

'It's a shithole,' replied Otis. 'Who the hell would come here?'

Ricky laughed. 'Not like this. We was gonna fix it up proper classy. But the council didn't give us no licence.'

'Good job. Would have been a waste of money.'

'That's what it is now,' Ricky admitted. 'Been up for sale since last year. No one wants it.'

'Can't understand that, Ricky,' Otis said sarcastically.

Johnny took my arm and dragged me over to a plastic chair. 'Sit,' he ordered.

I took a seat, trying not to shake. I heard a door clang open. Footsteps echoed across the stone floor. I looked up at Ricky.

'What do you want?' I asked.

Ricky shook his head and pulled a bag of cocaine out of his jacket pocket. Inside it was tiny silver spoon. He took a hit before handing it to Otis.

Johnny frowned. 'That shit is gonna kill you,' he told

him. 'Drive you nuts.'

'Like you ain't never done it . . .'

'Once in a while – I just don't fiend on it like you.'

Ricky swore at him.

'Fiend on what?' I heard Taz ask.

He was standing in the doorway, holding a can of Pepsi Max. His face was dark with stubble, his eyes wide. He was wearing a black suit, white shirt and pink tie.

'Where've you been?' asked Ricky.

Taz looked at me and grinned. 'Tying up some loose ends,' he said, his eyes fixed on mine.

I turned away, desperately thinking of a way out. The office was small, but if I could get past my captors, I might be able to reach the door. I was fast, and I didn't think Taz or Ricky could catch me. The problem was Johnny Owens and his gun.

'So,' said Taz, coming towards me, 'did you think you could bring me down?'

I didn't reply.

'Nothing to say now,' Taz said to Johnny. 'He couldn't *stop* talking before.'

Johnny came right up and leaned in to my face. 'We can *make* you talk. Otis can do that. Only it hurts… Not sure you'd like it.'

'What do you want?' I asked again, turning my face away from him.

258

Taz looked at me like I was crazy. 'You what? I don't *want* anything, Sat. I've got everything I need.'

'So why am I here?'

Taz crouched in front of me, so close that I could have broken his nose with one kick. *Could have* . . .

'Did you think we wouldn't find out?' he said. 'About you and that bitch?'

'What bitch?' I asked, my heart sinking.

'Don't play games, Sat,' he warned. 'I'm not in the mood.'

Johnny slapped me. The pain was intense, like a brick in the face. I felt my eyes water but I didn't make a sound.

'We know you and Laura stole things,' Johnny told me.

'Not that they help you,' Taz added.

I felt the anger rising inside me. Despite my situation, I wasn't going to show them how scared I was. I glared at him. 'They will when the police get them.'

Taz grinned. 'But you won't be talking to the police,' he told me. 'You're here, with us . . .'

I shook my head. 'Laura has copies of everything . . . And she's got the passport too. Anita's passport . . .'

I watched as Taz, Ricky and Johnny exchanged looks. I couldn't work out whether they were smirking or frowning.

Taz stood up, grabbed my face with his hand and

spat out his reply.

'*Laura?* She won't be talking to anyone.'

I tried to shake free but Taz held onto me, his fingers digging into my jaw.

'We had an agreement,' I told him, feeling more and more desperate. 'She'll go to the police if I don't meet her today.'

'Now that's a lie, isn't it, Sat?' Johnny said, mocking me. 'Because we spoke to Laura yesterday and she didn't mention that.'

Something fluttered in my bowels and I fought to keep control of myself. Laura . . .

'Don't worry though,' Taz added. 'You won't be seein' her no more – bit like your sister. Otis and Johnny done them both – reckon Jas was better. *That* bitch put up a fight—'

I kicked out with both feet then, landing one in Taz's midriff. He let go of me, stepping backwards. I pushed up, out of the chair, lunging for his throat. I didn't make it. My legs buckled beneath me as Johnny swept them away. He took hold of my neck from behind, stopping me from falling, and flexed the muscles in his arm. His fingers reached right around my throat. I felt them tightening, stopping the air. He held me like that for a few moments before flinging me down onto the chair again.

It tipped over and I hit the ground in a heap, tangled

up in chair legs. I tried to get up but Taz kicked out at my face – once, twice, until I felt the skin on my forehead break. Blood began to seep out, warm and wet against my right eyebrow.

'Pick him up!' I heard Taz shout.

Johnny grabbed my hair, pulling me to my feet. I swung a few punches but my fists bounced off him. He slapped me twice more, nearly knocking me out. I felt my legs going again.

'Sit him down,' ordered Taz.

Otis righted the chair and Johnny forced me to sit down again. This time Otis held me in place. Ricky was standing in the corner, snorting shit and giggling. I finally realized how crazy he was.

'Balls, man,' he said, winking at me.

I nodded. '*Big* balls,' I said, past the point of caring. 'Your mum loved them . . .'

I steadied myself for more violence but it never came. Taz intervened, blocking Ricky's path to me. He told me to stop making things difficult.

'For who?' I asked. 'Me, you or Jas? I don't care what you do to me – not any more . . .'

Taz slid a white A4 envelope, folded in half, out of his pocket. He unfolded it and took out some photographs.

'You don't care about yourself,' he said quietly, 'but you might care about these . . .'

He laid two of the photos in my lap, tapping them with

his forefinger. 'See?'

I looked down and saw my sister-in-law getting out of her red BMW 3-series. Behind her, in tall green letters, was the word ASDA. The second picture was Mandy again, only this time she was coming out of Asda with Aran in her arms. My brother was beside her, three bags of shopping in his hands.

'After our last little problem,' said Taz, 'I thought you might need *convincing*. I got Otis to follow them.'

On cue, Otis stepped forward and gave me a lopsided grin. 'Fine woman, that,' he said. 'Me an' her could hook up – easy.'

I shook my head. 'No!' I shouted. 'They ain't done nothing . . .'

Taz knelt down beside me. 'See?' he said. 'Any time we like, we can lift one, two or all three of them. We had to stop Otis from grabbing Mandy in the car park. He wanted to take her home and . . . what was it again, mate?'

Otis smiled. '*Mek she whine . . .*'

'*No!* I won't talk . . .' I begged, realizing that they had me.

'Up to you, Sat,' said Taz, ruffling my hair. 'But be warned, mate. The next person sitting here, if you say anything, will be that sister-in-law of yours. And who knows, we might have to bring the little kid along too . . .'

'Ain't no place for kids,' Johnny said. 'I seen rats in

262

here could eat a baby easy. Big, they are – like small dogs.'

'*I won't talk!*' I shouted. My head was spinning. I had to protect Mandy and Aran. I *had* to . . .

Taz smiled and stood up. 'That makes three of you, then,' he told me. 'You *won't* talk, Laura *can't* talk, and your sister – *well* . . .'

'What about my sister?' I asked frantically.

Taz knew that he had scared me. He knew that he had won. I was hoping that he'd tell me about Jas – explain what had happened to her. What did he have to lose? Only Taz didn't think that way.

'She ran off, mate,' he told me. 'Just like we said. And no one ain't seen her since.'

'Maybe she's with Anita.' There was a sneer on Ricky's face. 'Maybe she's sharing in that divorce payout that Anita thought she could steal from me!'

'Who knows?' said Taz.

'*Please* . . .' I begged. 'Tell me . . .'

Taz shook his head. 'We're leaving now. You wait until we're gone and then do what you like.'

'But—'

'Just remember,' Taz continued. 'You say *anything* to *anyone* and I'll feed your nephew to the rats – got it?'

I nodded as tears began to stream down my face.

'Good lad,' said Taz. 'I want the memory stick too.'

I shook my head. 'Don't have it,' I said, praying that

he wouldn't search me. The stick was in the left pocket of my jeans.

'Find it,' Taz ordered Johnny.

He got it first time, held it up.

'How stupid are you?' Taz asked me.

'I've got copies,' I said defiantly. Stupidly.

Taz grinned and picked up one of the pictures. He tapped it. 'One word,' he said. 'Just one word and we'll get the kid before the police get to us. I promise.'

I shook my head in despair. 'OK,' I told him. 'I won't talk . . .'

'I know.' He picked up the other photo too.

'Please just tell me about Jas,' I asked again.

Taz ignored me and left the office, the other two close behind. I waited a while before heading after them.

'Tell me what happened! PLEASE!'

My voice echoed around the warehouse, mocking me. I watched them disappear through the door. It clanged back against its frame as I fell to my knees, sobbing.

The white one pulled her up by the hair. Abused and bleeding, she whimpered like an injured animal. They stood in a clearing, the headlights from the car providing the only light.

'Where they at?' she heard the black man ask.

The moon hid behind clouds tinged with purple. The air was heavy, clinging to her, so humid you could almost taste it. Insects buzzed all around them. Somewhere close by, out in the darkness beyond the clearing, was a river. She felt herself drifting away, high into the Punjabi night sky, looking down on her own wretched existence. What was left of it.

She heard the clatter of a car engine in the distance. As it grew closer, she realized it was an old Jeep, battered and worn from years of use. It came to a stop beside her captors; two more men, both Punjabi, got out. One of them, short with dark greasy hair and an acne-scarred face, leered at her breasts. The driver was taller and wore a white turban. He spoke to her captors.

'Where is money?' she heard him ask in heavily

accented English.

'In the car,' replied the white man.

She watched as they moved towards it. The white man leaned in and pulled out a holdall. The driver of the Jeep took the bag, opened it and checked the contents. He seemed surprised.

'A bonus,' the white man told him.

'Get the things out of the Jeep!' she heard the driver shout to his companion.

'Do what you like with her,' the white man told him. 'But nothing left, yeah?'

'I understand,' replied the driver, turning to look at her.

'She's a fighter,' the black man said.

Once they were happy with the arrangements, the Englishmen left her with the Punjabis. The taller man set the bag down on the ground and approached her.

Once again she felt herself float away. When she looked down this time, they were pushing her through some bushes and down towards the riverbank. The taller one carried the holdall, the shorter, a sack, inside which she heard metallic items clanking together. She saw herself shuddering as the men threw her to the ground. From the sack they withdrew wooden-handled machetes, the blades shiny and well oiled. Each of them turned to her.

'Such a waste of beauty,' she heard the shorter man say.

The driver sneered. 'What is she – your sister?' he asked.

As she felt herself floating further and further into the night sky, she saw the first man swing down his blade, cutting deep into her stomach. The second man took aim and hacked at her face. As the men set about their task with greater purpose, she realized something strange. Despite it all, she had not uttered a single sound . . .

TWENTY-SIX

There wasn't a day, over the next two years, when I didn't think about Jas. When I didn't wonder what they had done to Laura. For the first few weeks I called Laura's mobile continuously. I never got through to her. Then I hung around her flat, to see if she would turn up. I *knew* it was pointless, *knew* that it made no sense because it was Taz's flat, but it was all I could do. Laura was gone, just like Jas and Anita, and it felt like it was my fault. I should never have gone after Taz. I should have known that I'd never be able to get him. The Atwals were always going to win – they were too strong, had too many people working for them.

My family tried to move on. Aran grew quickly, and by his first birthday Mandy was pregnant again. Each time I looked at her, I saw Otis Blackwood's eyes, his leering face. I recalled what Laura had told me: how he'd disfigured his ex-wife with acid. I saw Taz holding my nephew, laughing at me. Sneering arrogantly at my weakness – a man who knew he was untouchable. I had a scar above my right eye where Taz had broken the skin with his well-shined, hand-stitched shoe. I'd managed to explain it away – a drunken fall.

Dad went into retirement, letting Amar take over. He

looked worn; his eyes dull, white hairs appearing in his beard. He drank more and more, and spent his time sitting around or aimlessly walking the streets. Mum managed to keep busy, fussing over Aran and Mandy, but didn't go back to the *gurdwara*. Both my parents carried an invisible weight around with them: a sense of shame and dishonour that would never go away. No one mentioned Jas – not even me. Yet the more we ignored her, the heavier her presence became. She was always there, a ghost that haunted our lives, stopping us from truly moving on.

Amar was busy too, buying new shops and selling others. He went into property, using the funds Dad had saved up over a lifetime. He was successful and it seemed to make him happy. Yet sometimes, when I looked into his face, I saw that he was haunted too. Late at night, when he'd had a few drinks, his face gave him away. A distant look would enter his eyes and he'd go off somewhere inside his head.

Jas's room remained untouched. The only person to go in, other than me, was Mandy. She'd change the sheets and vacuum the hardwood floor, even though no one used the bed. Occasionally I sat at Jas's old desk, staring into space. I felt closer to her in that room – hoped that she might return some day. Only I knew she wouldn't, not ever.

* * *

The Atwals grew stronger. I watched from the sidelines as they opened more businesses, made more money, drove ever more expensive cars. I heard all the gossip. Johnny Owens was taking over the doors in Leicester. Taz and Ricky were bankrolling him. Otis Blackwood had beaten up this gangster or stabbed that bad bwoi. The Atwals bought a mansion out in the country. It had a lake, and gardens big enough to lose yourself in. They made the newspaper too. A local councillor was videoed in secret, offering planning information for cash. The article mentioned Taz but, as always, there was no evidence. Just the coincidence that Taz had bought up dilapidated properties in an area that later became a regeneration zone. The journalist who'd written the story was Jennifer Barton, still working despite an illness, still after them.

I saw them a few times, out in town. Once I was queuing to get into a club called Gyro, standing in the rain with a couple of girls I knew. A silver Range Rover Sport, the most expensive model, pulled up right by the doors. Taz and Ricky jumped out, wearing identical silver-grey suits, both with shaved heads. I watched them walk up to the doors like VIPs at a film premiere. The door staff shook their hands, patted their backs. Ricky pulled some women out of the queue, acting like a superstar. All he was missing was a red carpet and flashing cameras. I left the queue and went elsewhere.

On another occasion I was outside a bar called The Office, on a street packed with people. Taxis stood along every inch of the pavement. A black Mercedes S-class, the AMG with smoked windows, stopped a few metres away. The number plate read R1 CCY. The driver leaned on his horn, the other hand gesturing for a cabbie to pull out. The taxi driver stayed put, ignoring him. Then Ricky Atwal jumped out of the passenger seat and walked swiftly across. He kicked the taxi, denting the wing, and people gathered round to stare. The cabbie, an old Sikh guy in a pale green turban, got out and started cussing Ricky in Punjabi. Otis Blackwood emerged from the driver's side of the Merc, watching out for Ricky.

As soon as Ricky saw Otis, he slapped the driver. 'You know who I am?' he screamed at the old man. His eyes bulged.

The driver began to apologize, but Ricky smacked him a few more times, sending his turban flying.

'That ain't right,' someone behind me said. 'That Ricky Atwal ain't got no sense. Can't beat the man over dem tings. Man is old . . .'

'Someone should shoot that bastard,' someone else whispered.

The cabbie gathered up his turban and moved his taxi, allowing Otis to park in his spot. As the crowd began to break up, I shook my head.

'One day he'll get his,' I said quietly.

Only it wouldn't happen. Ricky, Otis and the others were too dangerous. No one messed with them. No one stood up to them.

My life stayed on hold. Each day I resolved to find a job, to get away. Yet by the evening I found myself doing the same things. Going out with lads I knew and getting drunk. Killing time at home, watching telly or surfing the Net. Amar made me work for my money, running errands for him. I could see my life slipping into the same routine as him and his mates – working for the family business, going out, weddings and functions. Until the day when I resigned myself to the future that was mapped out for me – married some girl my parents found, got fat and made babies. It didn't seem to bother Amar and his mates – it was what they'd expected from life. Only I'd always wanted more.

I was restless and bored. Most days I just existed, not making any plans, not caring. Dash moved to London, started at uni, and that just made things worse. Whenever I spoke to him or visited, I could tell that he was enjoying his life, meeting new people, going to new places. He told me about Charlotte and Pooja, about how well they were doing, how much they were enjoying university life, which only added to my frustration – even though I'd asked about them.

I just couldn't get on with things. My heart was filled with guilt and anger. I wished I could turn back the clock, warn Jas not to marry Taz. During imaginary fights, I battered his arrogant, smirking face. In vivid dreams, I met Jas in airports and train stations. She was alive and well, smiling that smile that I could never forget. It was like being stuck in a video loop. Over and over – the same feelings, the same thoughts. I thought my life would continue that way – a never-ending cycle of depression, guilt and anger. I accepted that I'd never find peace. Then, over two years after my last run-in with the Atwals, something changed.

I was in town, walking round the High Cross, when my phone rang. It was Dhaminder.

'Sat?'

'Yeah,' I replied, wondering why he'd called. We'd hardly spoken in two years – just the occasional stilted phone conversation.

A sense of dread invaded my thoughts. I heard a woman tut as I brushed past her, not watching my step. Several teenage lads stood outside Next, eyeing up girls. A kid was crying, her mum shouting.

'Where are you?' he asked, urgency in his voice.

'Why?'

'I'm in Leicester, Sat,' he explained. 'I know everything – about the evidence, *Laura* . . .'

My head began to spin. My heart fluttered as if thousands of butterflies were battering away inside my chest. The feeling reached my throat, and my mouth felt parched. How did Dhaminder know about Laura?

'You know that Time bar next to the station?'

'Yeah, I do.'

'Meet me there,' he said firmly. 'I'll be ten minutes. It's important.'

I listened, but his words didn't register. I was too busy thinking about Laura. For some reason the scent of her hair came flooding back. The way she looked, sitting cross-legged on her sofa, wearing light-grey jersey shorts and a white vest. The chocolate-brown mole just above her left collarbone.

'Are you still there, Sat?' Dhaminder asked.

'Yeah,' I told him. 'How do you know about—?'

'Just meet me,' he insisted. 'I'll tell you then.'

'In Time?'

'Yes.'

The place was half empty even though it was a Saturday afternoon. A large screen showed some golf tournament, a few people watching. The bar was long and narrow, widening out at the far end. I could smell brewing coffee, stale lager and bacon frying, and my empty stomach rumbled. I descended some steps, passed the toilets and found Dhaminder sitting at the bar. He was wearing a pale blue turban, black jeans, trainers, and a grey hooded top; in front of him was a glass of orange juice. I took the red stool next to his and sat down.

'You want a drink?' he asked, his eyes fixed on mine.

'Er . . .'

'You'll need it,' he said, his voice soft and unthreatening.

I'd been worried on the walk over. I was expecting him to be angry. If he knew about the evidence, he'd realize that I was a coward. That I'd run away from the Atwals, succumbed to their threats. But he didn't look mad at me. If anything, he seemed calmer than usual.

'Sat?'

'Yeah – I'll have a pint. Please . . .'

As Dhaminder got the barman's attention, I inspected the spirits behind the bar. They were displayed in colour order, from clear vodkas through to the darkest of rums. The bottles were backlit and they glinted. The black sambuca caught my eye.

'Here,' said Dhaminder, pushing a pint towards me.

'Thanks.' I picked up the glass and took a swig.

Dhaminder sipped his juice. 'How've you been?' he asked.

'OK,' I said with a shrug. 'Just getting on with things. How about you?'

He shrugged back at me. 'You know . . . Just trying

to keep going – running the website and chasing for clues in India.'

I looked away, felling guilty. I wondered why he was stalling. He knew about the evidence, so why wasn't he angry? He should have been asking questions, bouncing me around the room in rage. Not exchanging pleasantries and buying me drinks. His calm demeanour made no sense.

Dhaminder coughed and looked at the barman. 'You should have told me,' he said as soon as the man walked away.

I put down my drink and looked at him. 'About what?'

'*Sat* . . .' he said, unblinking. 'You found evidence about Anita. You and Laura . . .'

I nodded. 'Yeah, but how do you know? The only people that know are me, Laura and the Atwals. *I* didn't tell you, the Atwals wouldn't have, and Laura—'

Someone tapped me on the shoulder. I turned round and my heart nearly stopped beating.

'Hello, Sat,' said Laura, with a huge grin.

TWENTY-SEVEN

We took a cab to my house. The driveway was empty apart from Mandy's BMW, the red paint gleaming.

'Are you sure about this?' Laura asked.

From the moment she'd tapped my shoulder, I'd been sure.

'Yeah,' I said, taking her hand. 'I thought you were dead.'

Laura gave me a hug, whispering in my ear. My heart was pounding, electricity buzzing around my head. I couldn't believe that she was alive. I'd spent two years thinking that Taz had hurt her . . . killed her. Two years in which I'd mourned her almost as much as I had Jas. And here she was. The pit of my stomach grew warm and I had to fight back tears of joy.

'I'm sorry,' she told me. 'I'm *so* sorry . . .'

Dhaminder coughed, nodded towards the door. Mandy was standing in the porch looking bemused. Aran was with her, tapping on the glass. Laura let go, her face red.

'That's my sister-in-law,' I told them.

Mandy opened the door, smiled and asked me to introduce my friends. Aran called to me, his arms outstretched. I picked him up and turned to his mum.

'Laura and Dhaminder,' I told her. 'Where's everyone else?'

'Amar's sorting out paperwork at the chippy. Your mum and dad are round at Uncle Preet's.'

'Call Amar,' I said. 'He needs to come home.'

I led Laura and Dhaminder into the house. Aran seemed fascinated by Dhaminder's turban and beard. He arched across my shoulder, trying to get a better look.

'Here,' I said to Anita's brother. 'Have him.'

Aran gurgled in delight as Dhaminder took him. We went through to the kitchen, which smelled of fresh curry.

'Have a seat,' I told them, turning back to Mandy.

'What's going on?' she asked me.

'Please, Mandy,' I begged. 'Just trust me. Call Amar and tell him to come straight home.'

Mandy beckoned me into the hallway. 'That girl,' she whispered, 'is she your girlfriend?'

I shrugged. 'Dunno,' I said honestly. 'But she used to go out with Taz Atwal.'

Mandy's eyes widened; her face turned the colour of her BMW. 'She went out with *Taz*?' she asked, her surprise evident.

I nodded. 'All through his marriage to Jas . . . Before, and after too.'

'But—' she began.

'Just call Amar,' I said. '*Please?*'

Amar was back within twenty minutes, his face flushed, his eyes blazing. I didn't hear what Mandy had said but it worked. He was wound up, and only the sight of Dhaminder playing with Aran stopped him from losing it.

'This better be good,' he warned me, eyeing Laura. 'Is this the girl?'

Mandy nodded.

'Why are you here?' Amar snapped at Laura.

'Because I invited her,' I replied, stepping in front of her. 'We've got evidence that proves the Atwals are guilty.'

Amar looked to me, surprise etched across his face. 'The Atwals?' he asked.

'Yeah,' I said. 'And this time you're going to listen.'

Dhaminder kicked off, filling Amar in on his experiences with Ricky. He told him all about Anita and the reasons why he'd become suspicious.

'A man in India admitted that Anita had been murdered,' he said. 'But when the British police went over, he'd moved away. The Atwals own everyone in their old village. No one talks about them. They bought the villagers off or scared them away. But I know my sister didn't run off with anyone.'

Amar and Mandy listened closely, occasionally

glancing at each other. Then Dhaminder showed them Anita's passport.

'Laura found this in a safe at Dice,' he said. 'Why would my sister run off without her passport?'

'You found this?' Amar said to Laura.

'Yes,' she replied. 'I found photos of Taz, Ricky and the others in India too. The dates coincide with Anita's disappearance.'

I sat down between my brother and Laura. 'Tell him everything,' I said to her.

Laura sighed and asked me for some water. As I went to fetch it, she told her story too. I added bits as she went along, explaining my part in things. After nearly forty minutes Amar and Mandy knew almost everything.

'Do you see now?' I asked my brother.

He nodded, hands on the table, the veins thick like green worms.

'Every bit of Taz's evidence against Jas was a lie. Azhar Khan didn't exist – Taz invented him. And now, with what we've got, the police can reinvestigate. Maybe Jas tried to leave him. Maybe she found out what they'd done to Anita.'

'And I'll be a witness, if you need me,' Laura added.

'Why are you helping us now?' Amar asked her.

Laura looked at me.

'This didn't happen recently,' I told my brother. 'We found out two years ago.'

282

Mandy stood up, holding Aran against her shoulder. 'Why wait so long?'

'Because no one listened to me,' I said bitterly. 'I *tried* to talk to all of you. But you took Taz's word instead. All that *shit* about honour . . .'

Amar looked like he wanted to cry. He shook his head slowly. 'But you could have shown us this stuff,' he said.

'I couldn't. Taz threatened to hurt you. He had pictures of you, Mandy and Aran. He said he'd kidnap you—'

'*Me?*'

'*All* of you. He even threatened to kill Aran. I couldn't tell anyone. I couldn't risk Aran . . .'

Amar's jaw grew tight. He pushed himself away from the table, stood up. '*What?*'

'Amar, don't shout,' said Mandy. 'You'll scare the baby . . .'

Amar looked at his son and blinked slowly. 'I'm gonna kill him . . .' he murmured. 'I'm gonna ring the lads, go round there and—'

'You *can't*,' said Laura. 'You don't know them. Otis and Johnny like to hurt people. And they've got serious backup too.'

'I don't care,' Amar insisted. 'They don't scare me.'

Mandy went over and placed a hand on his back. 'Think about your son. If something happens to you, what do I tell Aran?' She looked down at her pregnant belly. 'What do I tell the new one?'

Amar turned to me and shook his head. 'I'm sorry,' he said. 'I should have listened to you.'

I shrugged. 'Yeah, you should have.'

Dhaminder cracked his knuckles, then spoke up.

'We've got no choice,' he said. 'It's the police or nothing. We can sit around all day and talk but it won't help us.'

I agreed. 'Nothing ain't an option. We can't let them get away with this.'

'There's no proof about Jas,' said Amar. 'Only what Laura says.'

'No,' I said, feeling a renewed sense of urgency. Something I hadn't felt for two years. 'But we *can* get them – even if it's just for tax.'

Laura put her hand in mine. 'I'm sorry . . .' she said.

Mandy smiled at her. 'It's not down to you.'

'Yes it is – partly, at least. I shouldn't have helped Taz.'

Amar sat down again. 'We can't change that now,' he said. He looked at me and repeated my words: 'We *can* get them, though.'

The kitchen door creaked open, and I saw my parents standing there. They eyed us suspiciously. My mum clearly found Laura particularly interesting.

'What's going on here?' Dad asked in Punjabi.

I looked at my brother. 'Amar?' I asked, hoping that he'd talk to them. Explain what we were doing. I'd done a lot of thinking over the previous two years, grown up a bit . . . Just not enough to forgive my parents. I didn't want to explain. It would have made me too angry.

Amar nodded and stood up. 'I'll deal with it,' he told us, heading for the door.

TWENTY-EIGHT

'They can get to us,' I told Amar, two days after he'd spoken to Dad. We were in his car, driving to one of his rental properties.

'Not if they've been arrested,' he pointed out, turning onto a main road.

I frowned. 'Let's say they arrest Ricky . . . Taz finds out. He'll send Johnny and Otis out before we know it. We can't risk that.'

Amar considered my words for a moment. In front of the car, an Eddie Stobart lorry blocked the road. The driver was trying to turn right, into a narrow side street. Cars parked on both sides prevented him from doing so.

'So what do we do?' he asked, braking.

'I've got a plan,' I told him. 'I want you to take the family away. Go and stay with someone—'

'Why?'

'Because they can't *get* what they can't find.'

'I'm not running,' Amar said defiantly. 'Let them come.'

I shook my head. 'You're not listening. Otis and Johnny won't go down from a slap or two. They've got guns, Amar. They're psychos.'

'But—'

'*No!* I'm not putting anyone at risk. They've already hurt Anita and Jas. No way are they getting to Mandy or Aran.'

Amar seemed to calm down at the mention of his son. He stared straight ahead, watching the lorry's manoeuvres. 'So what's the plan?'

'The journalists who helped write the story . . .'

'What about them?'

'I spoke to Jennifer Barton this morning,' I said. 'She's really sick, but she gave me a number for Amanda Ryan.'

'How does that help?'

I watched a motorcyclist weave in and out of the traffic jam ahead. 'Amanda works for a national newspaper now. I'm gonna tell her what we've got. See if she'll help us.'

'But we can just tell the police,' Amar pointed out.

'I want to get it all down. Then we can hide while the police do their thing.'

Amar looked surprised. 'You're *that* scared of the Atwals?' he asked.

I nodded. 'Yeah . . .' I fingered the scar Taz had given me, feeling no shame. 'They'll kill all of us, given half a chance. Taz threatened to feed Aran to the rats. And he sent Otis to follow you all. They're capable of anything.'

Amar's face clouded over. 'OK,' he said. 'I get your point.'

The lorry driver was still unable to move. I told Amar to let me out of the car. 'I can walk,' I said. 'Do a U-turn and go back. No point being stuck here all day.'

Amar nodded, releasing the auto door-locks on his S-class. 'You'll be OK?' he asked as I let myself out.

'Yeah,' I replied. 'I wanna talk to Laura. I'll be back later, maybe.'

Amar grinned at me. '*Maybe?*'

I swore at him and walked away.

Laura took me up to her room, closing the door behind us. 'My old bedroom,' she said.

The room was big, with a huge bay window that overlooked the rear garden. A double futon lay to the left, opposite the chimney and a Victorian fireplace. The walls were deep red and seemed to close us in. To the right of the door was a desk and rows of bookshelves.

'Nice,' I said, sitting down on the futon.

'Everything OK?' she asked, joining me. She wore wide-legged black trousers, a tight grey T-shirt and white trainers. Her hair was still damp from the shower.

'Yeah,' I said. 'I just feel odd, seeing you.'

She looked at me and smiled.

'How did you get away?' I continued. 'I called your mobile for weeks. Why didn't you let me know?'

'I couldn't,' she said. 'Taz threatened my family.'

I stared at her. 'How did he know where you were?'

'He didn't. He sent me an email with a picture of my mum leaving the house. They photographed my sister coming out of school, and my brother with his mates in Burger King. He even got someone to break in and take a photo of my bedroom. I was scared.'

'I know how that feels,' I admitted. 'When I saw the pictures of Mandy and Aran, I went cold inside.'

Laura nodded. 'When they came for me at the flat, I climbed out of the bathroom window,' she explained. 'I dropped onto a flat roof and jumped into someone's garden. All the houses have alleyways, so I ended up on Edward Road. I lost my phone escaping and I couldn't go back for it.'

'And you took off?'

'Yeah, I drove to Birmingham in the Mini.'

'Why Birmingham?'

Laura leaned back against the wall, crossing her legs. 'I wanted to find you, Sat,' she said. 'But I didn't know where you lived. I decided to go and see my dad. He runs a guest house in the Lake District. I dumped the car at New Street station and got a train.'

'So when Taz had me in the warehouse . . . ?'

Laura nodded. 'He lied, yeah.'

'That was risky,' I said.

'I guess so – but it worked,' she replied.

I leaned back too, my thigh brushing her knee. 'You climbed out the *window*?'

Laura grinned at me. 'I'm a resourceful lady,' she said. 'Besides, what choice did I have? Otis and Johnny . . .'

She didn't finish her sentence because there was no need. We both knew what would have happened if they'd caught her. I thought it *had* happened.

'I was so scared,' she said, straightening her legs and leaning towards me.

Her scent, sweet and musky, made me feel warm inside. I put my hand on her thigh, felt the heat from her skin.

'Why did you come back, then?' I asked softly.

She looked into my eyes. 'The same reason you can't stop thinking about Jas,' she said. 'It's not like I forgot, Sat. The guilt was killing me. I couldn't sleep properly or concentrate. I was angry too – with Taz. I thought he'd beaten me, won. After a while I couldn't take it any more.'

'But *two years*?' I said.

Laura sighed. 'The emails didn't stop at first,' she told me. 'He sent one every month. I'd call Mum and she'd tell me he'd been round, asking after me. He even sent flowers on my birthday. My mum told me I was crazy to leave him – he proper charmed her. I couldn't tell her the truth.'

'So what changed?'

'I dunno. The emails stopped coming. I waited a

couple of months and then I thought about contacting you. I found Dhaminder's website and left him a message. It sort of went from that . . .'

I nodded.

'I could have just got your number and called,' she added. 'But Dhaminder wanted to see you too.'

'I thought he'd be angry about it,' I said.

'Yeah, me too. He's the calmest man I've ever met.'

'Unlike me,' I murmured.

She moved closer still. 'So did you forget about me?' she teased.

'Yeah,' I joked. 'You're *so* forgettable.'

I heard a door slam and voices on the stairs.

'That'll be my mum,' said Laura, getting up. 'Come on – she wants to meet you.'

'I want to meet her too,' I replied. 'I've got a plan.'

As I stood up, stretching my legs, Laura asked what I had in mind.

'I'm gonna speak to Amanda Ryan – the journalist who helped write about Anita and Jas.'

'The one from the *Mercury*?'

'Yeah – but she's with a national paper now.'

Laura looked confused. 'Why speak to her first?'

'Because I'm worried about the Atwals.' I repeated what I'd said to Amar, outlining my plan in full. I wanted everyone who mattered to be out of Taz's reach.

'Where can we go?' she asked.

I shrugged. 'Anywhere . . . But you can't stay here. Not until they're all locked up. Come on, Laura, you know what they'll do.'

She shuddered. 'My mum is gonna go ballistic . . .'

'Don't worry,' I said, taking her hand. 'I'll back you up.'

Laura kissed my cheek gently. 'I've really missed you,' she said.

'Me too,' I replied. 'Come on – let's get this over with.'

Amanda Ryan picked at her food. The more she'd heard of my story, the more slowly she'd eaten.

'Where are Laura and the others now?' she asked me.

'Safe. Somewhere the Atwals can't get at them.'

Amanda shook her head. 'I still don't understand why you waited so long. The tax evidence alone will get them sent down.'

'You don't understand because you can't,' I told her. 'They would have got to us . . . to our families. They're dangerous people. If someone threatened your family – proved that they could hurt them – what would you do?'

This time Amanda's face changed. She looked at me and nodded. 'I see what you mean.'

'It's easy to say call the police,' I went on. 'But when you're in that situation, faced with people like Johnny Owens and Otis Blackwood, you feel helpless – useless. Your personality changes. Every knock on the door is scary. Every passing car is a threat . . .'

I didn't need to finish what I was saying.

'And now?' asked Amanda. 'What's changed?'

I looked away, out of the window, watching the rain that had started to fall. 'Guilt,' I replied. 'I've spent two years trying to forget, but it's no good. There's no cure for it. Either I'm stuck with this for ever or I do something. I try to change things.'

'And what about Laura?'

'The same thing,' I said. 'She's angry too, mostly with herself.'

Amanda asked me what I wanted to do next.

'Write the story,' I told her.

'I have to call the police first. It's my duty to tell them what I know . . .'

I nodded. 'We've still got all the evidence.'

'The police can protect you too,' she added. 'I'm sure they can.'

I shrugged. 'All it takes is for one of them to stay free,' I told her. 'Ricky, Otis, Johnny — doesn't matter.'

Amanda shifted in her seat, picked at some cold rice. 'So why come to me?'

'I wanted backup. Last time the coppers fobbed me off. I tried Jennifer, but she's really ill — I guess you know she's got bowel cancer . . . she gave me your number. If you write up the evidence and present it to the police — they'll have to take it seriously.'

Amanda sighed when I mentioned Jennifer and her illness. I could see how gutted she was.

'She's not going to make it,' she told me. 'I speak to her regularly. They've given her a few months at most.'

'I know,' I said. 'I went to see her yesterday. She told me to give you a message.'

Amanda's eyes quizzed my face. 'What message?'

'She said to make sure that you hang 'em high,' I replied.

Amanda's eyes instantly filled with tears.

'What does it mean?' I asked.

'Jennifer is the best investigative journalist I've ever met,' she said. 'She would have been great at a national but she didn't want to move her kids. She taught me to check and recheck my information, get the best evidence, and never trust sources until you'd really sussed them out. She taught me how to get the bad guys too. Hang 'em high . . . like she did – racist coppers, corrupt politicians, dodgy directors, gang lords – whoever . . .'

'So are you gonna help?' I asked.

Amanda looked thoughtful for a few moments, wiping away her tears. 'I'll have to,' she joked. 'Otherwise Jen is going to kill me. She's been after the Atwals for years.'

'Thank you.'

Amanda looked away. 'No, Sat. Thank you. This is going

to be a good story.'

'Yeah . . .'

'Oh God!' she said. 'I didn't mean that . . . I wasn't belittling your pain.'

'It's OK. It's just horrible knowing that it won't help Jas, that's all.'

'Have you still got DI Elliot's number?' she asked me.

'Yeah, but it's two years old.' I handed her my mobile phone.

She took it from me and smiled as she scrolled through my address book. 'I bet she answers.'

I grinned. 'If she does, I'll eat every fish head I left on my plate . . .'

'You're on,' she replied, making the call.

It took seconds.

'Hi, DI Elliot? This is Amanda Ryan . . . Yes . . . I used to work with Jen Barton . . .'

I looked at the greasy cold fish heads on my plate and shook my head.

Derby Evening Telegraph, 17 August

MAN QUIZZED OVER ANITA ATHWAL DISAPPEARANCE

Detectives re-investigating the disappearance of Derbyshire woman Anita Athwal are to question a new suspect.

Police arrested the unnamed man in Leicester late last night. Officers are also questioning three other men.

A spokeswoman for Derbyshire Police said that they had received new information in the case, prompting a fresh inquiry. Anita Athwal vanished while on holiday over five years ago . . .

Leicester Mercury, 17 August

LOCAL MAN ARRESTED IN CONNECTION WITH MISSING WOMAN CASE

Leicestershire Police last night arrested an unnamed local man in connection with the disappearance of a Derbyshire woman.

A spokesman for Leicestershire Police said that the force would be working closely with their Derbyshire counterparts. Three other men, all local, are also being questioned.

The missing woman, Anita Athwal, disappeared more than five years ago. A source told the *Mercury* that new information has prompted a fresh investigation into the case.

Leicester Mercury, 19 August

THREE MORE ARRESTED OVER ATHWAL CASE

Three more local men have been arrested as the Anita Athwal case gains momentum.

Police raided three addresses in the city last night, as part of an ongoing investigation. The arrests came just two days after police detained a fourth suspect. All four men remain unnamed . . .

Derby Evening Telegraph, 20 August

MAN CHARGED WITH ANITA MURDER

A man has appeared at Derby Crown Court, charged with the murder of missing local woman Anita Athwal.

Rajinder Atwal, 32, of Leicester, is also charged with abduction. He has been remanded in custody, to appear in court on 2 September. Derbyshire Police are still questioning three other men in a joint investigation with their Leicestershire counterparts.

Anita Athwal has been missing for over five years and members of her family are said to be 'delighted' at the latest turn of events.

'My sister's case has been ignored for too long,' said her brother, Dhaminder Singh. 'Finally Anita might get the justice she deserves.'

Leicester Mercury, 21 August

THREE MORE CHARGED WITH ANITA ATHWAL MURDER

Police today named three more men charged with the abduction and murder of a missing woman.

John Owens, 36, Otis Blackwood, 41, and Taswinder Atwal, 29, all from Leicester, appeared at Derby Crown Court. All three were remanded in custody, to appear again on 2 September.

A fourth Leicester man, Rajinder Atwal, has already been charged with the same offence. Police gave few further details and investigations continue . . .

Guardian, 29 August

BRITISH POLICE FLY TO PUNJAB IN MURDER INQUIRY

Officers from the East Midlands flew to Punjab in India yesterday, as they widen their investigation into the abduction and murder of Anita Athwal from Derbyshire. Meanwhile Mrs Athwal's brother questioned police handling of the case and claimed that his sister's race may have led to police inaction.

Mrs Athwal, who vanished more than five years ago, was last seen in the Hoshiarpur region of Punjab. A spokesman for Derbyshire Police told reporters that the local Indian force had offered their help in investigating the case.

'We are confident that, between us, we can learn the truth about Mrs Athwal and her murder,' said the spokesman.

Four men, all from Leicester, have been charged with Mrs Athwal's abduction and murder, including her husband, Rajinder Atwal – whose surname, inexplicably, is spelled differently to that of his wife. As community groups in both Derby and Leicester question police failings in the case, the missing woman's brother revealed serious misgivings about the case and police handling of it.

'I told them five years ago,' claimed Dhaminder Singh. 'They weren't interested back then, and it's taken this new evidence to finally wake them up. My family and other interested parties are going to demand an inquiry once the trials have taken place. It seems to me that my sister's life meant nothing to the police. If she'd been white, none of this would have happened.'

The suspects are due to appear in court next week . . .

Leicester Mercury, 1 September

POLICE INVESTIGATE SECOND MISSING WOMAN CLAIM

Police investigating the Anita Athwal case are today beginning a new inquiry into a second missing woman from the same family. The latest developments come just one day before four men are due in court, charged with Mrs Athwal's murder.

Jaswinder Atwal, 22, from Leicester, went missing nearly three years ago. Her husband, Taswinder Atwal, stands charged with the abduction and murder of his sister-in-law, Anita Athwal. Mr Atwal, a well-known Leicestershire businessman, denies all charges.

'We have received further credible information which has prompted us to open an investigation,' said Detective Inspector Elliot of Leicestershire Police. As yet no charges have been brought in this new case.

Local community leader Piara Singh Bains spoke of his shock at the latest developments.

'We know the families,' he said. 'It is terrible what is going on. The police have a duty to clear up this matter urgently. The community is in shock at this.'

Meanwhile a local domestic abuse charity today claimed that both cases highlighted a serious issue within Leicester's Asian community.

'These cases are tragic,' said Jagdeep Cheema of 'Speak Out'. 'But we all know that such things happen in our community. It is time for the elders, the so-called leaders, to make a stand against such things. Too many women are scared to speak out.'

Police issued no further comment when questioned.

Derby Evening Telegraph, 2 September

MURDER SUSPECT FOUND DEAD IN CELL

A murder suspect was found dead in his cell last night, just hours before he was due to appear at Derby Crown Court.

Rajinder Atwal, from Leicester, stood accused of the abduction and murder of his wife, Anita Athwal, of Derby.

Police gave few details when questioned, other than the dead man's name. However, they did rule out foul play. Initial findings pointed to 'death by natural causes', according to a police spokeswoman.

Guardian, 14 November

SECOND VICTIM MYSTERY DEEPENS IN ANITA ATHWAL CASE

Police in the Anita Athwal case seem no closer to resolving the fate of a second woman, thought to be related to the first victim by marriage.

Jaswinder Atwal, married to Mrs Anita Athwal's brother-in-law, disappeared in Leicester nearly three years ago. The police were slow to investigate her case, relying instead on the story given to them by her husband, Taswinder Atwal. Mr Atwal claimed that his wife had run off with another man after a lengthy affair.

Subsequent inquiries have failed to find Mrs Atwal or her supposed lover.

As more details emerge, the mystery deepens. Despite a difference in the spelling of their surnames, both Anita Athwal and Jaswinder Atwal were married into the same family, to brothers. Both brothers, along with two other men, were charged with the abduction and murder of Anita Athwal. Hours before a second scheduled court appearance, Rajinder Atwal, husband of Anita, was found dead in his cell. A post-mortem established heart failure as the cause of death.

'It's too much of a coincidence,' said Melanie Lawton-Singh from the women's charity 'Shanti'. 'That two young women have vanished from the same family is beyond belief. The police should have picked up on the problem much sooner. Had they acted when Anita's brother first spoke to them, Jas Atwal might never have disappeared.

'It is obvious to anyone with a shred of common sense that the Atwal family has a case to answer. Two missing women, two similar stories, and two brothers in the thick of it.'

A spokesman for Derbyshire Police urged caution when questioned. 'It is unwise to make accusations until court proceedings have finished,' he said. 'We are aware of the sensitive nature of this case within the victims' communities, but we must not get carried away. We are working with our counterparts in India and in Leicester to gather the evidence we require. Our inquiries will be thorough and exhaustive.'

Leicester Mercury, 19 February

GUILTY VERDICTS IN ANITA ATHWAL MURDER

Cheers and tears greeted the verdicts handed down in the Anita Athwal case at Derby Crown Court.

John Owens, Otis Blackwood and Taswinder Atwal, from Leicester, had denied all charges against them. Yet it took the court just under an hour to convict all three with the abduction and murder of Anita Athwal.

The men, who between them stand charged on seven other counts, will be sentenced later.

Mrs Athwal's brother, Dhaminder Singh, from Derby, burst into tears as the verdicts came in. Mr Singh had fought a near five-year campaign to bring justice for his sister.

'I was overwhelmed,' he later said. 'The Atwals told so many lies about Anita – lies that the police fell for. It was just such a relief to see them pay. I feel that my sister has had her dignity returned today and I want to thank everyone involved. I just hope that the Jaswinder Atwal case can also bear fruit.'

Jaswinder Atwal, wife of Taswinder Atwal, went

missing nearly three years ago, in circumstances similar to those of Anita Athwal. Yet, whereas Anita's family have found peace, the investigation into Jaswinder's whereabouts continues . . .

Guardian – G2, 25 May

KILLING HONOUR

Amanda Ryan

Satinder (Sat) Kooner lets a second coffee grow cold as he tells me about his missing sister, Jaswinder. We sit in Caffè Nero just round the corner from St Pancras International as the public rush by, most of them unaware that an epidemic of abuse and murder goes largely unreported, ignored by the mainstream media.

The murders, dubbed 'honour killings' by some, happen in closed, tight-knit ethnic-minority communities, in cities and towns across the UK. Official figures suggest that up to 17,000 women in Britain are subjected to honour-related physical and mental abuse, sexual assault, and, in extreme cases murder, every year.

Sat Kooner bristles with rage when I bring up the subject. His eyes, ringed with dark circles, show the pain he evidently feels. He exudes a world-weariness that one might expect in a forty-something, yet he is still a teenager.

'Even when they do report it, the media call it "honour killing" or "honour-related abuse", which is a joke. Those murders aren't about honour – more like killing honour. If thousands of white British women faced that sort of abuse, the response would be different.'

I mention the thousands of women and girls of every background who experience domestic abuse each year, and Sat calms down a little.

'I don't mean to turn it into a race thing,' he adds. 'But sometimes it does feel like it. I often wonder what would have happened if Jas had been white. Would we have got a better response from the police and the media?'

Jaswinder Atwal (formerly Kooner), from Leicester, was known to family and friends as Jas. A beautiful and shy teenager, she was studying to become a beautician when rumours of a secret boyfriend enraged her parents, offending their ideas of family honour and Punjabi tradition. Pulling Jas away from her course, her parents arranged a marriage to Leicester-based businessman Taswinder Atwal.

'She was so respectful,' Sat explains, his eyes moist. 'There was nothing she wouldn't do for my parents, you know? Even if they upset her, she'd still honour them. She gave them so much respect and they let her down.'

Ten months into her marriage, Jas vanished. The Atwal family claimed that she'd run off with a lover, citing Facebook pages and text messages as proof. The rest of the Kooner family accepted Taswinder Atwal at his word, but not Sat.

'They made up some Muslim boyfriend,' he tells me. 'They knew that my parents would freak at that – the whole Sikh/Muslim thing. Taz Atwal knew that my dad would feel ashamed and disown Jas. And that's exactly what happened. Taz played us from the start.'

I ask him why his father would have reacted badly to a Muslim lover in particular.

'Sikhs generally marry Sikhs,' he explains. 'And Muslims mostly stick with other Muslims – it goes back to the partition of Pakistan and India – the tensions between the two religions – maybe even further back, I dunno. I *do* know that the Atwals used that tension to get what they wanted.'

Unable to rest until he'd discovered the truth behind his sister's disappearance, Sat began to investigate, giving up any normal teenage life he might have had, including his place in school. He set up an online campaign to find his sister, using every social networking site he could find and posting her details on numerous websites. One of many Internet searches eventually revealed the story of Anita Athwal, a case that had made national headlines earlier in the year. Sat quickly realized that his suspicions were correct.

'Anita was married to Ricky Atwal, Taz's brother.

She'd vanished too, in almost identical circumstances. The more I found out about Anita's case, the more certain I was that the Atwals had hurt Jas. I got in touch with a journalist who'd covered Anita's story – and with you. That led to Dhaminder Singh, Anita's brother. The rest is what it is. Just like it's been reported.'

Despite learning the truth about Anita, Sat felt unable to contact the police immediately. I ask him why and his face grows pale.

'We found out loads,' he begins. 'I even met someone who could be a witness. But I was fighting against two things. Firstly, my family wouldn't listen to me. They were too caught up in feeling ashamed. Their concept of "honour" is so ingrained that they couldn't take my sister's side. They just swallowed what Taz Atwal told them. I was much less grown up back then, and their support would have helped me to make the right decisions. But I was on my own and I made mistakes.

'The other thing was Taz Atwal,' he explains. 'He threatened me a few times, but that was easy to get over. I didn't care what happened to me. I just wanted to find out about Jas. But when Taz started to threaten my family, I got really scared. He'd sent some thugs to follow my brother and his family. He even threatened to feed my baby nephew to rats. Then the witness I'd found vanished too. I gave up.'

He excuses himself and goes to the bathroom. When he returns, his eyes are red. I ask about how he felt when the Atwals finally paid for their actions.

'It was weird,' he says. 'I was so pleased for Anita's family and relieved that Taz couldn't hurt anyone else. When I found out that Ricky Atwal had died in prison, I had a drink to celebrate. But it was Anita's case that got settled, not my sister's. I still don't know what happened to her.'

When I ask how this lack of closure has affected him, he shrugs and looks away. It is some time before he feels composed enough to reply.

'Well, I don't feel like a normal teenager. I don't do what regular teenagers do,' he tells me with a warm smile, behind which lurks an obvious sadness.

'It just hurts,' he adds. 'I mean, I've thought about it over and over again. I still daydream about Jas being alive. I imagine that she's going to walk through the door any minute. Only I know that can't happen. As soon as I found out that the Atwals had killed Anita, I knew that Jas was dead too. I just couldn't admit it to myself.

'The other day I was watching telly and they showed a re-run of *Ugly Betty*. My sister loved that show – made me watch it with her. I wanted to talk to her, you know? I wanted to eat pizza and ice cream and talk rubbish. She's never coming back, though, is she?'

I ask if he'd like to finish up, worried that my questions might add to his sorrow. He shakes his head.

'I feel like I have to talk about her,' he explains, with another melancholy smile. 'There's this big hole in my life and it's never gonna be filled. Taz Atwal won't talk so we'll never know what really went on. We'll never be able to put her to rest; never know why Taz killed her. And that's disrespectful to Jas and her memory. She deserves more than that. So, for me, talking about her keeps her alive and gives some respect back. I know that sounds weird but it's how I feel.

'And there is some good that's come from this,' he adds. 'It's brought my family closer together. My parents understand what really happened now. It hasn't helped them become less depressed, but at least I can relate to them now. They thought I was trying to dishonour them by searching for Jas. Now they know it was the opposite. I was trying to honour my sister. They just couldn't see it.'

BALI RAI

Killing Honour is Bali's eighth young adult book for RHCB. His first, *(un)arranged marriage,* created a huge amount of interest and won many awards, including the Angus Book Award and the Leicester Book of the Year. It was also shortlisted for the prestigious Branford Boase first novel award. *Rani and Sukh* and *The Whisper* were also both shortlisted for the Booktrust Teenage Prize. Bali also writes the popular Soccer Squad series for younger readers.

He was born in Leicester, where he still lives, writing full-time and visiting schools and libraries to talk about his books.

You can visit him at **www.balirai.co.uk** and turn over to read Bali's thoughts on some of the issues raised in *Killing Honour.*

Your book focuses on 'honour killings', which are often linked to situations where girls or women behave in a way that their traditional families find extremely shameful or dishonourable; for example, starting a relationship with someone from a different culture, or asking for a divorce. In these cases, the families of the women are often involved in their deaths. However, in *Killing Honour*, both Jas and Anita are actually murdered by their husbands for financial reasons. Did you deliberately choose to make their situation different?

Yes, I deliberately chose not to focus on actual honour killings. Instead, I decided to explore how the idea of 'honour' affected the families involved. Why would the parents disown the women? And how would the situation affect the siblings? I've always been shocked and amazed by the idea that family members can commit or collude in honour-based violence and, in many cases, remain quiet as it occurs. This was the angle I wanted to explore.

What inspired you to write *Killing Honour*? Was it a specific case or story, or the more general issue of honour killings?

I've always found the term 'honour killing' strange. It seems to imply murder based on mitigating circumstances to me, rather than just murder. It's a very odd term. Honour-based violence, including murder, affects thousands of women and men around the world. Whenever I hear about, or read of, such incidents in the UK I get angry that it occurs. The story that first grabbed my attention was the case of Kiranjit Alhuwalia in 1989. She killed her husband in self-defence, after a decade of abuse, but was sent to prison for murder. Various groups took up her case and she was eventually released from prison on appeal. My story 'Beaten', for the *Walking A Tightrope* anthology, was inspired by her case. Honour-based violence has also occurred in my extended family in the past, which added to my desire to write about it.

Have you ever known anyone personally who has experienced this?

Yes. Three female members of my extended family have experienced honour-based violence, rather than murder. Having said that, one of them committed suicide as a result and the other two women were forced to flee their homes. There may be others too, who just haven't spoken of their experiences or have simply accepted them – that wouldn't be uncommon. It is something that that I feel deeply about.

Why do you think honour killings still happen in Britain, even when the families involved generally lead Western lives?

It's not a simple question to answer. Honour-based violence and killings in the UK happen because many of the old traditions are still held onto by people from South Asian communities. I think that the integration that I went through hasn't happened for many others from my background. About half of my family, when I was growing up, only led Western lives outside of the home, when they *had* to. In social terms they stayed amongst their 'own' and refused to integrate, and most still do. I remember older people saying that we shouldn't become 'too white', and that we'd always be outsiders in the UK.

The issue is more pertinent in the current climate, with people like David Cameron questioning multiculturalism in the UK. For me, many people don't *get* what a multicultural society is about. It seems to me that it's about differences first, when I think we should celebrate what we have in common. We are all British first and any differences simply add to that, which is wonderful. As a kid I didn't see differences first. My mates and I were just British kids from different backgrounds, all growing up together. Certain people don't understand that for whatever reason. The whole issue has become a hot potato and is something I could talk about for hours.

In the book, you have included scenes where a woman is beaten, and then eventually killed. Did you have Jas in mind when you wrote these scenes – or Anita, or both?

With those scenes I wanted the reader to decide. I wanted them to feel a little of what Sat was feeling. He has no idea what happened to his sister but imagining what might have happened is perhaps even worse than knowing the truth. For me they fit both Anita and Jas, but I wanted the readers to think about the circumstances that both women might have found themselves in. Initially they were about Anita but as the story grew, it became apparent that Jas was in there too. It's funny that writing works that way sometimes. Things come to you as you write which weren't there during the planning stage. It's one of many reasons why I love it so much.

On page 138 you describe 'a great wall of silence' in the community around the disappearance of a girl. How powerful are the community's actions in affecting the behaviour of Jas's family? Would they really have to stop going to the gurdwara, for instance?

The concept of honour in British Asian communities centres on the way others perceive your family. Anything that is seen to be dishonourable can affect that. That pressure, for many, is very great. People tend to keep things in the family, rather than air their problems in public. It is something that would affect Sat's family deeply. The idea that they've lost face would stop Sat's mum from going to the gurdwara, simply because she'd think others were talking about her.

The silence is there too – most people of my background can tell at least one story of a girl who has left home, run away or otherwise shamed her family. But on the whole, the community doesn't talk about it. Refuges for British Asian women are not widely supported or even discussed.

Jasvinder Sanghera, who wrote the novel *Shame*, often talks about how hard it is to change minds. The Kiranjit Alhuwalia case is another example. I had an argument with a male cousin over it. He sided with her husband, even though this man had beaten his wife for years. Male domination is deeply ingrained in Indian culture and, by default, in parts of British Asian culture too. Husbands are regularly supported over wives, and the community as a whole just seems to accept that. It is something that angers me greatly.

What sort of research did you do when writing the book?

Apart from reading about cases of violence and murder, I also thought back to situations that occurred in my own family and community. Then, once I'd planned the story, I started to put myself in Sat's shoes. How did he feel about his sister's disappearance and his family's reaction to it? What was he going to do about it? I considered the motives and actions of the Atwal's too – but not to the same extent. For me, Sat and his family were always the main focus; the divide between his family's traditions, which are very Indian, and his own British Asian experience. Sat is a natural progression for me, from Manny in *(un)arranged marriage*, both main characters in *Rani and Sukh*, and Simran and David in *The Last Taboo*.

Are any of the characters in the book based on real people?

Yes. I always base my characters on real people. Sometimes it's only their physical characteristics but often it's their personalities too. The reactions of Sat's parents are based on the older generation of my family – their traditions and ideas about family and honour. Sat's brother is a mix of different people I know, as are many of the other characters.

Is the character of Sat anything like you were as a teenager?

Yes – in terms of how he thinks, and his dislike for some of his family's traditions. I always found myself battling to be British with many in my family, who saw themselves as Indians first. I've always been much more

British Asian than Indian – and that's only natural as I was born and raised in the UK. That's a conflict that affects many people from my background, and it's the conflict that drove *(un)arranged marriage*, *Rani and Sukh* and *The Last Taboo*, as well as *Killing Honour*. The books are a natural progression for me.

When you were growing up, did you ever feel torn between Asian and British values? What was the most difficult thing for you?

I was always torn between Indian and British values. I was constantly told that India was my home but it never felt that way. India was always somewhere else, and I was much happier, and felt more at home, in England. There is a massive difference between British Asian culture and that of India – neither is better than the other – just different. I've always felt British first, and that's something that has caused issues for some of my family. I'm not the only one though.

**Also by Bali Rai and
available from Corgi . . .**

Torn apart by violence, united by love . . .

It's 1919 and Amritsar is a city on the brink of violent rebellion.

Bissen fought bravely for the British Empire during World War One. Now he patiently awaits news from England.

Gurdial, a young orphan, is desperate to marry Sohni, the daughter of a rich and evil man.

And Jeevan, Gurdial's oldest friend, is swept up in the revolution and changing beyond all recognition.

Bissen, Gurdial and Jeevan are trying to escape ghosts from the past. But as the fight for Amritsar reaches a terrifying climax, their lives will be changed for ever.

'Powerful storytelling . . . constantly surprising, beautifully compelling' *Scotsman*

*Manny wants to be a footballer. Or a musician.
Or write a bestseller. He doesn't want to get married . . .*

Manny is on his way to a wedding – his wedding.
A wedding that he doesn't want, that he
never asked for. To a girl he doesn't know.

At seventeen, Manny wants to do his own thing, to
choose his own path in life. But will his traditional
Sikh family's expectations be too strong to fight?

**'Absorbing and engaging . . . a highly readable
debut from Bali Rai that teenagers of any culture
will identify with'** *Observer*

Sometimes names can lead to terrible trouble . . .

The Punjab, 1950s. A secret affair goes horribly wrong,
and a young girl commits suicide after her lover is attacked
by her family. The two families part in violence and conflict.

Leicester, 2004. Rani and Sukh fall in love,
unaware of the terrible legacy of the past and the
dark history between their ancestors.

Can tragedy be averted this time, or will the
couple be drawn into the bitter cycle of enmity
that has gripped their families for years?

**'Frustratingly honest and overwhelmingly powerful . . .
a heart-wrenching love story that will exert its power
over you long after the book is finished'** *The Bookseller*

*'Mess with one of us – then you have to deal
with all of us . . .'*

Positive attitudes only. That's the Crew: Billy,
Jas, Della, Will and Ellie. And where they
live – in the concrete heart of a big city –
you need a crew to back you up.

Then one day they find a fortune in notes –
and life suddenly becomes very dangerous . . .

'A jewel of a book' *Independent*